THE BRIGHTON BOYS WITH THE SUBMARINE FLEET

BY

JAMES R. DRISCOLL

The Brighton Boys with the Submarine Fleet

CHAPTER I

GOOD-BY, BRIGHTON

"Wanted: young men to enlist in Uncle Sam's submarine fleet for service in European waters."

The magic words stood out in bold type from the newspaper that Jack Hammond held spread out over his knees. Underneath the caption ran a detailed statement setting forth the desire of the United States Government to recruit at once a great force of young Americans to man the undersea ships that were to be sent abroad for service against Germany.

Stirred by the appeal, Jack snatched the paper closer and read every word of the advertisement, his eyes dancing with interest.

"Your country needs you now!" it ran; and further on:

"The only way to win the war is to carry it right home to the foe!"

Below, in more of the bold type, it concluded:

"Don't delay a moment—-while you hesitate your country waits!"

From beginning to end Jack read the appeal again. Before his eyes in fancy flashed the picture of a long, lithe steel vessel skimming the ocean, captain and crew on the lookout for the enemy, the Stars and Stripes flapping from the tailrail. For an instant he imagined himself a member of the crew, gazing through the periscope at a giant German battleship—-yes, firing a torpedo that leaped away to find its mark against the gray steel hull of the foe!

Up in the dormitories some chap was nimbly fingering "Dixie" on the mandolin. The strains came down to the youth on the campus through the giant oak trees that half obscured the facade of "old Brighton." Over on the athletic field a bunch of freshmen "rookies" of the school battalion were being put through the manual of arms by an instructor. Jack could hear the command: "Present arms!"

"I guess that means me," he said to himself. And why not? Hadn't Joe Little and Harry Corwin and Jimmy Hill left school to join the aviation service? Weren't Jed Flarris and Phil Martin and a bunch of Brighton boys in Uncle Sam's navy? And hadn't Herb Whitcomb and Roy Flynn made history in the first-line trenches? Yes, the boys of Brighton were doing their bit.

In another moment Jack had crushed the newspaper into his pocket—-his decision made—-jumped from the bench under the old oak tree and was speeding across the campus in the direction of the main dormitory entrance.

Without waiting for the elevator he leaped the steps, three at a time, running up to the third floor, and thence down the corridor to No. 63—-his "home," and that of his chum, Ted Wainwright.

Out of breath, he hurled himself into the room. Ted was crouched over the study table, algebra in front of him, cramming for an examination.

"There you are! Hip, hurrah!" Jack cried excitedly, thrusting the folded newspaper under Ted's eyes and pointing to the bold typed appeal for recruits, all the while keeping up a running fire of chatter.

Ted was in the midst of a tantalizing equation. He was accustomed, however, to such invasions on the part of his chum, the two having lived together now for nearly three school years—-ever since they had come to Brighton.

Both boys were completing their junior year in the select little school for which the town of Winchester was famous. They lived at remote corners of the state and had met during the first week of their freshman year. They had found themselves together that first night when the "freshies" were lined up before the gymnasium to withstand the attack of the "sophs" in the annual fall cane rush. Together they had fought in that melee, and after it was all over, anointed each other with liniment and bandaged each other's battle scars.

Jack was a spirited lad, ready always for a fight or a frolic, impetuous and temperamental; Ted had inherited his father's quiet tastes and philosophical views of life, looking always before he leaped, cautious and conservative. So, when Jack came bouncing in, gasping with excitement, Ted accepted the outburst as "just another one of chum's fits."

"What's all the grand shebang about this time?" he queried, shoving the algebra aside and taking up the newspaper that had been thrust upon him.

"I'm going—-I'm not going to wait another minute—-all the other fellows are going—-my grandfather fought through the Civil War—-it's me for the submarine fleet—-I'm off this very——-"

But before he could ramble any farther Ted took a hand in the oratory.

"What's the matter, chum? Flunked in anything, or been out to see a new movie show, have you?"

Jack ran his finger down the newspaper column to the advertisement for recruits.

"There you are!" he shouted. "And what's more, I'm going to sign up this very afternoon. What's the use of waiting any longer? Here's a great chance to get out with the submarines—-think of it!—-and, gee, wouldn't that be bully? Look! Look! What do you say, old boy; are you going with me?"

Jack's enthusiasm "got" Ted. Taking up the newspaper he read every word of the appeal, slowly, deliberately. Then he looked up at his chum.

"Do you mean it, Jack; are you in earnest?" he asked, after a long pause.

"Never meant anything so much in all my life," was Jack's quick rejoinder.

For an instant the two boys faced each other. Then out shot Ted's hand, clasping that of his room-mate in a firm grasp.

"Well, chum, I guess we've been pretty good pals now for nearly three years. You and I have always stuck together. That means that if you are going in, I'm going too!"

"Great!" bellowed Jack with a whack on the back that made Ted wince.

"Let's beat it quick for the recruiting station. Are you on?"

Hat in hand he bolted for the door, but stopped short as Ted interrupted:

"Don't you think we'd better tell the home folks first?"

The impetuous Jack turned. "I hadn't thought of that."

"Of course we will," answered his chum. "We'll send them a telegram right away, telling them we are going to enlist tomorrow."

It was agreed, and no sooner said than done.

There was not much sleep in 63 that night. Long after lights were out the two boys were huddled together in their den, gazing out at the stars and speculating on the new adventure for which they were heading.

The morning train into Winchester brought among its passengers two very much perturbed mothers and two rather anxious fathers. The Hammonds and Wainwrights had met in the spring during commencement week festivities and had much in common this morning as they came together in the Winchester terminal. Ted and Jack were at breakfast when word was brought to them of the presence of their parents in the president's reception room.

It was a joyful little reunion. Only a few minutes' conversation was necessary, however, to prove to the parents that each of the boys was dead in earnest in his announced intention to enlist in the navy.

"I don't suppose there is much to be said here," concluded Ted's father after listening to the son's impassioned appeal for parental sanction. "You seem to have decided that you owe allegiance to your country above all other interests. I shall not interfere. As a matter of fact, my boy, I'm proud of you, and so—-here's God bless you!"

Jack's father felt the same and so expressed himself. Only the two little "maters," their eyes dimmed with mist, held back; but they, too, eventually were won over by the arguments of the eager lads.

It was decided that the party should have dinner together in town and that in the afternoon the boys would present themselves for examination at the recruiting station. The remainder of the morning was spent in packing up belongings in 63 and preparing to vacate the "dorms." The boys decided to wait until after they had been accepted before breaking the news to their school chums. Each felt confident of passing the necessary requirements. They had made the football team together in their freshman year. Jack had played, too, on the varsity basket-ball team for two seasons, while Ted excelled on the track in the sprints.

Dinner over, the entire party repaired to the recruiting station. It did not take long to get through the formalities there and, needless to say, each lad passed with flying colors.

"All I want to make sure of," ventured Jack, "is that we get into the submarine service. I'm strong for that, and so is chum."

There was a twinkle in the eye of Chief Boatswain's Mate Dunn, in charge of the recruiting station.

"I reckon Uncle Sam might be able to fix it for you," chuckled the bronzed veteran. "He's fitting out a great submarine fleet to get right in after the Prussians, and, since you fellows seem so dead set on getting there, I guess maybe it'll be arranged."

Jack and Ted were in high spirits, and eager to be off for the naval base at once. Officer Dunn had informed them they might be forwarded to the nearest navy yard that night with a batch of recruits signed up during the week. He told them to report back to the recruiting station at seven o'clock "ready to go."

The boys were anxious, too, to get back to Brighton and break the news. It was arranged they should spend the dinner hour at the school bidding farewell and later meet their mothers and fathers at the recruiting station.

There was a great buzz of excitement in the mess hall at dinner when the news spread that Jack Hammond and Ted Wainwright had enlisted in the navy and were soon to leave. As the bell sounded dismissing the student body from dinner, Cheer Leader Jimmy Deakyne jumped up on a chair and proposed three cheers for the new recruits. And the cheers were given amid a wild demonstration.

Out on the campus the boys had to mount the dormitory steps and make impromptu speeches, and then submit to a general handshaking and leave-taking all around. "Fair Brighton" was sung, and the familiar old Brighton yell chorused over and over, with three long 'rahs for Jack Hammond and three for Ted Wainwright.

"Makes a fellow feel kinda chokey, don't it, chum?" stammered Ted as he and Jack finally grabbed their bags and edged out through the campus gate.

They turned for another look at old Brighton. The boys were still assembled on the dormitory steps singing "Fair Brighton." Up in the dormitory windows lights were twinkling and the hour hand on the chapel clock was nearing seven.

"Come on, chum, let's hurry," suggested Jack. They walked in silence for a moment.

"Pretty nice send-off, Jack," sniffed Ted, finally. "We'll not forget old Brighton in a hurry."

"And you bet we'll do our best for Uncle Sam and make old Brighton proud of us," added Jack.

At the recruiting station all was lively. The boys were told they must be at the depot ready to leave on the seven-thirty express. A score or more lads were waiting for the word to move, some of them taking leave of their loved ones, others writing postcards home. Ted's folks were waiting; Jack's came along in a few minutes.

A special car awaited the recruits at the railway terminal. The girls of the Winchester Home Guard had decked it in flags and bunting and stored it with sandwiches and fruit. In another ten minutes the express came hustling in from the west. A shifting engine tugged the special car over onto the main line, where it was coupled to the express. All was ready for the train-master's signal to go.

"Good-by, mother; good-by, dad," the boys shouted in unison as the wheels began to turn and the train drew out of the train shed. A throng filled the station, and everyone in the crowd seemed to be waving farewell to some one on the train. The Winchester Harmonic Band had turned out for the send-off to the town's boys and it was bravely tooting "Stars and Stripes Forever."

Soon the train was creeping out into the darkness, threading its way over the maze of switches and leaping out into the cool country air. All the boys were in high spirits, mingling boisterously in jolly companionship, the car ringing with their songs and chatter.

Jack and Ted lounged together in their seat, chatting for a while; and finally, when the tumult had abated and the boys were getting tired, dozing away into slumber to dream about the new world into which they were being carried.

Behind them, Winchester and Brighton! Before them, the stirring life of "jackies" aboard one of Uncle Sam's warships—-bound for the war zone!

CHAPTER II

DOWN IN A SUBMARINE

Daylight found them rolling through the suburbs of a great city. The long night ride was nearing an end.

All around them as their train wended its way through the railway yard were evidences of the unusual activities of war times. Long freight trains were puffing and chugging on the sidings; the air was black with smoke, and the tracks filled everywhere with locomotives and moving rolling stock.

In a few minutes the train slowed down into the railway terminal and the score or more of "rookies" were soon stretching their legs on the platform. A detail of blue jackets, spick and span in their natty uniforms, awaited the party. Jack and Ted stared at the fine looking escort, thinking what a wonderful thing it would be when they, too, were decked out ready for service in such fine-looking attire.

They had not long to wait. Breakfast over, the entire party boarded trolley cars bound for the navy yard. Soon, across the meadows, loomed the fighting tops of battleships, and in the background the giant antennae of the navy yard's wireless station.

"Here we are at last, chum!" chortled Ted with a broad grin, as he and

Jack piled out of the car.

Passing the armed sentries at the gate, the party of recruits were marched first to the commandant's office, where their arrival was officially reported. After roll call and checking up of the list of names, the boys were all marched over to the quartermaster's depot to be fitted for uniforms. Probably the most impressive moment of the morning to the boys was the ceremony of swearing them into service—-when they took the oath of allegiance to their country.

Jack and Ted were anxious to get into their uniforms and were afforded an opportunity very shortly when they were directed aboard the training ship Exeter, where they were to be quartered for a few days until detailed into service on one of the fighting units in the yard.

The first few days aboard the Exeter passed rapidly, the time being so filled with drills that the boys had few idle moments. Their letters home and to their chums at Brighton contained glowing accounts of the new service into which they had entered.

After a week of it they were standing one afternoon on the forecastle of the Exeter watching the coaling of a giant dreadnought from an electric collier when a naval officer, immaculate in white linen and surrounded by his staff, came aboard. After an exchange of salutes between the deck officer of the Exeter and the visiting officer, and a brief chat, the recruits were ordered to fall in. The naval officer in white stepped forward.

"You boys will be distributed at once among the vessels now in the yard to make up the necessary complement of crews. The department is very anxious to put some of you aboard the submarine fleet now fitting out here, and if there are any in the crowd who would prefer service in the submarines to any other service you may state your preference."

Jack and Ted stepped forward immediately. Other boys followed suit. And so it came about that Jack Hammond and Ted Wainwright found themselves detailed to the U.S. submarine Dewey.

A young officer approached and introduced himself. "I am Executive Officer Binns, of the Dewey. If you boys are ready we will go right aboard. We expect to go down the bay on some maneuvers this afternoon and want to get you fellows to your places as quickly as possible."

The whole thing was a surprise to Ted and Jack. They had expected to be kept in the yard a long time, quartered on the training ship. To get into active service so soon was more than they anticipated.

Marched across the navy yard they soon came in sight of the Dewey—-a long cigar-shaped castle of steel, sitting low in the water, riding easy at the end of a tow line near the drydock. Up on the conning tower a member of the crew was making some adjustment to the periscope case, while from astern came the hum of motors and the clatter of machinery that bespoke action within the engine room below.

"Looks like a long narrow turtle with a hump on its back, doesn't it?" whispered Jack as he and Ted came alongside.

They were passed aboard by the sentry and there on the deck welcomed by the officers and members of the Dewey's crew. Turned over to big Bill Witt, one of the crew, they were directed to go below and be assigned to their quarters.

Down through the hatchway clambered Witt, followed close by Ted and Jack, and in another moment they found themselves in the engine room. Electric lights glowed behind wired enclosures. Well aft were the motors and oil engines, around them switchboards and other electrical apparatus—-a maze of intricate machinery that filled all the stern space. The air was hazy and smelled strong of oils and gases. Huge electric fans swept the foul air along the passageway and up through the hatchways, while other fans placed near the ventilators distributed the fresh air as it poured into the vessel, drawn by the suction.

From the engine room the boys walked forward into the control chamber—-the base of the conning tower—-the very heart and brain of the undersea ship. Here were the many levers controlling the ballast tanks, Witt explaining to the boys that the submarine was submerged and raised again by filling the tanks with water and expelling it again to rise by blowing it out with compressed air. Here also was the depth dial and the indicator bands that showed when the ship was going down or ascending again, the figures being marked off in feet on the dial just like a clock. Here also was the gyro-compass by which the ship was steered when submerged; here also the torpedo control by means of which the torpedoes were discharged in firing. And, yes, here was the periscope—-the great eye of the submarine—-a long tube running up through the conning tower twenty feet above the commander's turret of steel.

"Something like the folding telescope we have at home to look at pictures," mumbled Jack aside to Ted.

To the boys' great delight they were allowed to put their eyes to the hood and gaze into the periscope. In turn they "took a peep." What they saw was the forward deck of the Dewey, the guns in position, other vessels moored nearby and the blue expanse of water stretching out into the harbor and on to the open sea. It was rather an exciting moment for the two "landlubbers."

Witt next showed them forward through the officers' quarters and the wireless room into the torpedo compartment. This interested them greatly. On either side of the vessel, chained to the sides of the hull on long runners that led up to the firing tubes, were the massive torpedoes, ready to be pushed forward for insertion in the firing chambers. Chief Gunner Mowrey was working over one of the breech caps and turned to meet the new recruits.

"Glad to meet you, mates," was his hearty salutation.

The boys listened attentively while Mowrey was telling Witt of some great "hits" they had made in practice earlier in the morning. Bill Witt showed the boys in turn the bunks that folded out of the sides of the vessel in which the crew slept, the electric stove for cooking food in the ship's tiny galley, the ballast tanks and the storage batteries running along the keel of the vessel underneath the steel flooring.

Climbing up on deck again through the conning tower, the boys found themselves out on top of the projection in what Witt explained was the deck steering station whence the Dewey was navigated when cruising on the surface. Down on the deck the boys inspected the smart-looking four-inch guns with which they later were to become better acquainted, and the trim little anti-aircraft guns to be used in case of attack by Zeppelins or aeroplanes.

"Keep your eyes and ears wide open all the time; remember what you are told and you'll soon catch on," Witt told them.

Shortly before noon Lieutenant McClure, commander of the Dewey, a youthful-looking chap who, they learned later, had not been long out of Annapolis, came aboard. It was soon evident that there was something doing, for in a few minutes the propeller blades began to churn the water, and the exhaust of the engines fluttered at the port-holes. The tow lines ashore were cast off and then very gracefully and almost noiselessly the Dewey began slipping away from its dock. The head of the vessel swung around and pointed out the harbor.

"We're off, boy!" exclaimed Jack to his chum. They were, indeed. The boys were standing in front of the conning tower and, because it was their first submarine voyage and they had yet to acquire their sea legs, they kept firm hold on the wire railing that ran the length of the deck on either side of the vessel. Commander McClure and Executive Officer Binns were up on the deck steering station behind a sheath of white canvas directing the movement of the ship.

"This is what I call great!" laughed Ted as the Dewey began to gather speed and moved out into the bay.

Looking seaward the boys beheld the prow of the submarine splitting the water clean as a knife, the spray dashing in great white sheets over the anchor chains. From aft came the steady chug-chug of the engines' exhaust, to be drowned out at intervals as the swell of water surged over the port-holes. They seemed to be afloat on a narrow raft propelled swiftly through the water by some strong and unseen power.

"I say, old boy, this beats drilling out on the campus at Brighton with the school battalion, eh? what?" exclaimed Jack.

Ted was doing a clog dance on the deck. "I'm just as happy as I can be," was his gleeful comment.

Very shortly the lighthouse that stood on the cape's end marking the harbor entrance had been passed and the Dewey was out on the open sea. Before the boys stretched water—-endless water as far as the eye carried—-to the far thin line where sky and water met. They were lost in contemplation of the wonderful view. But their reveries were suddenly disturbed by a sharp command from Executive Officer Binns:

"All hands below—-we are going to submerge!"

The Dewey was going to dive!

CHAPTER III

SEALED ORDERS

Ted and Jack hastened to follow their comrades down the hatchway. A seagull flapping by squawked shrilly at them as the boys waited their turn at the ladder. Instinctively they took another look around them before dipping into the hold of the Dewey. They realized that here, indeed, was the real thrill of submarining. The cap was lowered at last and secured, and the crew hastened to their posts amid the artificial light and busy hum of the ship's interior.

Now the Brighton boys were to learn how the Dewey was to be submerged! For one thing they noted that the oil engines used for surface cruising were shut off and the locomotion of the vessel switched over to the electric drive of the storage batteries. But their attention was directed chiefly to Navigating Officer Binns, who had taken up his position before a row of levers and water gauges amidships.

"Pump three hundred pounds into No. 1," was the command given by Binns. One of the levers was thrown over, and immediately could be heard the swirling of water. The boys were unable to grasp the full meaning of what was going on until Bill Witt shuffled up and said: "I'll put you fellows wise to what's going on, if you want me to."

Ted and Jack were glad to know what it was all about and listened attentively to the commands of the navigating officer and the interpretations given by their new-found friend. Bill explained that the process of diving was called "trimming" in submarine cruising, and that the pumping of the water being directed by Binns was done to fill the ballast tanks, thus increasing the displacement of the Dewey and causing it to settle in the water. First one tank was filled, and then another, until the vessel was submerged on an even keel. This was a revelation to the boys, for they had supposed it was only necessary to tilt the ship and dive just like a porpoise.

To their great delight the recruits found that the Dewey, like other submarines built since the beginning of the great world war, was equipped with twin periscopes, and that, furthermore, they would be allowed to watch the submersion of the Dewey through the reserve periscope if they so desired. Would they care to? Well, rather! For the next few minutes they took turn about peering into the mirrors that reflected the whole panorama before their eyes.

Gradually, they could see, the Dewey was settling into the embrace of the sea. Now she was down until the waves rolled completely over the deck and splashed against the conning tower. Down, down they dropped till only the periscope projected above the waves. Before them stretched the wide sweep of water, the ocean rising slowly but surely to overwhelm them. One after another the waves surged by. Now the eye of the periscope was so close to the crest of the water that it was only a matter of another moment until they would be under. Up, up, up came the water to meet them. Ted's heart was in his mouth while he viewed this awesome spectacle. Then he gave way for Jack to take a squint through the tube that carried with it a last look at the world of sunlight they were leaving. And now the eye of the periscope was so near submersion that the swell of the waves swept over it and momentarily blotted out the light. Then the spray dashed madly at the "eye" of the tube--and they were under!

Down in the depths of the ocean! It was a moment to stir the pulses of the two Brighton recruits. Wide-eyed in wonder, tense with the strain of the experience, they stepped back from the periscope. Through Ted's mind flitted memories of Jules Verne's "Twenty Thousand Leagues Under the Sea," and he was suddenly inspired to find out whether it was possible to glimpse any of the wonders depicted by the writer. A peep into the tube showed only a greenish haze as the rays of the sun seemed trying to follow the Dewey into the depths. Against the eye of the periscope streamed a faint flicker of greenish particles in the water that reminded the boy of myriad shooting stars. And then--nothing but a blur of black!

"What do you know about that?" gasped Ted, turning to his old school pal. The boys were keyed to a high pitch by this time as a result of their first experience in a deep-sea dive. So tense were they with excitement that they marveled at the care-free attitude of the crew. Some of them were humming nonchalantly; others chatting and laughing as though on an excursion on a river steamboat.

"What do you feel like, chum?" began Ted, as the two settled into a conversation over their wonderful exploit.

"Well, I've been up in the tower of the Woolworth Building and down in a coal mine and up in a Ferris wheel and once I had a ride with Uncle Jim in the cab of a locomotive--but this beats anything I ever had anything to do with!" exclaimed Jack, all in one breath.

Ted was gulping a bit. "I feel as though I had left my heart and stomach up there on top of the ocean," he stammered.

Bill Witt grinned from ear to ear; the remark was reminiscent of other "rookies" and their first experiences at sea.

"You'll probably think you've completely lost some parts of your department of internal affairs before you get rightly acquainted with your new friend Mr. Neptune," offered Bill by way of a gentle reminder.

So far the new members of the Dewey's crew had been unaffected by the terrors of seasickness. Bill's remark drove the import of it home pretty hard. "I hope, if we are going to get it," interjected Ted philosophically, "we get it soon and get over with it."

They had little time to ponder over the possibilities of gastronomic disturbances, for there was much going on that occupied their attention. The Dewey was now running entirely submerged, testing out her electric batteries.

"How do they steer the vessel down here under the sea?" asked Jack.

"By the gyrocompass," answered Bill Witt, pointing to where Executive Officer Binns and Commander McClure stood in the conning tower. "We are running blind down here, except that the skipper knows from his compass which direction we are going, and he has charts that tell him the depth of the sea at this point. They know the longitude and latitude and can easily determine on their maps and charts just where we are."

"How deep down can we go?" inquired Ted.

"Most of the boats have to be tested at a depth of two hundred feet before they are accepted by the government from the builders," replied Bill. "But you can bet your life we don't often go down that far. When we do, the water is oozing through the thin steel hull and dropping in globules from the sides and top of the vessel. From sixty to a hundred feet is our average plunge."

Even at that moment the boys noticed that the Dewey was "sweating" a little bit, the vaulted steel above them, coated with a composition that contained cork, being dotted here and there with drops of water. Jack craned his neck to look at the depth dial and noted the indicator hand was pointing at seventy-two feet.

Mess was served at noon while the Dewey kept on her run. Coffee and biscuits made up the frugal meal this time, the officers and crew being anxious to prove the submersible ready for any emergency call that Uncle Sam might make, and not desiring to spare the men from their posts longer than possible.

All afternoon the Dewey ploughed the waves, sometimes running submerged, other times on the surface. About five o'clock the boys perceived the lighthouse at the bay entrance, and soon they were back in the navy yard. Their letters home that night thrilled with accounts of their first dive under the ocean, and in their dreams the boys were sharing all manner of wonderful exploits against the foe on the boundless sea.

For several weeks the Brighton recruits were kept busily at the business of mastering submarine navigation. In the distribution of the crew throughout the vessel Jack and Ted found themselves assigned under the leadership of Chief Gunner Mowrey. In turn the boys were drilled in the forms for loading and firing torpedoes from the chambers in the bow of the boat, and in manning the four-inch guns above deck, as well as the anti-aircraft guns that poked their noses straight up in the air and sent up shells much after the fashion of Fourth of July skyrockets. The crew had pet names for their guns. The forecastle gun was nicknamed "Roosey" for Colonel Roosevelt, the gun aft was dubbed "Big Bob" in honor of "Fighting Bob" Evans of Spanish-American War fame, while the anti-aircraft guns became "the Twins."

"Hope we get a shot at a zepp some day soon with one of the Twins," sighed Jack one afternoon after the gun crew had finished peppering to pieces a number of kites that had been raised as targets.

"Yes, and I hope we get that shot at the zepp before the zepp gets one at us," replied Ted, as he recalled the stories he had read of the submarines being visible while yet under water to aircraft directly overhead, and thus being a ready target for a sky gunner.

Coming in the next afternoon from a run to shake down the engines, the boys on the Dewey found the navy yard in the vicinity of the submarine fleet moorings in a commotion. Motor trucks were depositing piles of goods near the piers which were being lightered to some units of the submarine fleet in motor launches. Officers were hurrying to and fro between their vessels and the shore and there was a general air of suspense that seemed to indicate early action of some kind.

The Dewey was wigwagged to take up a position near the other undersea craft that were being provisioned and fueled, and very soon supplies were coming aboard.

"Looks like we are going away from here," suggested Ted to his sailor comrade.

"It's a guess I've been making myself," answered Jack.

Their surmises were all too true, for very soon Commander McClure, who had been ashore for some hours now while the businesslike preparations were in progress, came alongside in the launch of the commandant of the yard and called his staff of officers into executive conference down in the officers' quarters. The news spread quickly through the Dewey as though by magic, that the submarine was due to get away during the night under sealed orders. A few minutes later Bill Witt confirmed the news. He was on night watch and had heard it from the officer of the deck.

Under sealed orders! Where and what!

CHAPTER IV

SOMEWHERE IN THE NORTH SEA

The Dewey was off! Shortly after midnight the little craft got under way, with her nose pointed out of the harbor.

"I guess it's 'so long U.S.A.' this time," confided Jack to his chum, as they stood together, aft the conning tower.

"Gee, I'm glad we're off!" answered Ted. "I only hope we are going over there with the rest of the boys."

Although they had yet to learn officially their destination, the Brighton boys, together with other members of the crew of the Dewey, took it for granted they now were on their way to Europe to join the great American fleet and battle with the Imperial German Navy for the mastery of the sea. It had been noised about ever since their enlistment that Uncle Sam's submarine fleet was soon to be sent abroad.

"Going to fight the U-boat snakes with made-in-America snakes!" was the way Bill Witt had sized up, the situation one evening when he and the Brighton recruits had been discussing the likelihood of their getting out on the firing line at an early date.

Jovial Bill Witt had proved such a capital good fellow that Jack and Ted had taken a great liking to him. The three boys were great pals by this time and were always together in their leisure moments. Temperamental Jean Cartier, the smiling little Frenchman who had shipped aboard the Dewey as chief commissary steward, very often joined their circle and spun the boys stories of that dear France and his home near Marseilles.

To-night it was different. There was no levity. Every man seemed to sense the situation and stood to his post of duty grimly conscious of the serious business upon which he had embarked. Through the minds of the lads flitted visions of home and campus.

Jack, dreaming of good old Brighton, was stirred out of his reverie by his chum.

"Do you suppose we will go all the way over under our own power, or will we be towed?" Ted was asking.

"Haven't the least doubt but that we'll stand on our own sea legs," replied Jack. "Don't you remember how we read in the papers early in the war of a bunch of submarines put together in the St. Lawrence River going all the way across to Gibraltar and thence through the Mediterranean to the Dardanelles under their own power?"

Ted did remember, now that it had been called to his mind. It had gripped their imagination at the time; it seemed such a wonderful thing, the fact that submarines small enough to be carried on the decks of huge liners had been able to cross the Atlantic alone and unaided. They had been still further amazed by the feats of the German undersea cargo carrier Deutschland that had made the trip to America and back, and the U-53 that suddenly popped into Newport one summer afternoon.

The night dragged along. Now that they were fairly off, Jack and Ted preferred not to sleep, but rather to keep tabs on the maneuvers of the American fleet. The sea was calm and the Dewey cruised on the surface, with her hatches open. The boys were able to stretch themselves in a promenade on the aft deck and found the night air invigorating as they speculated together on their mission.

They had soon to find out something of the number and character of warships in the fleet of which the Dewey was a unit. As daybreak came stealing up over the horizon they looked about them to discern many other warships all about them. Far to port, strung out in single file about a half mile apart, were three huge liners that they took to be troopships. Deployed around them were destroyers—-four of them—-riding like a protecting body guard. Bobbing about at intervals in the maritime procession were other submarines, their conning towers silhouetted against the dim skyline.

Relieved of duty, Jack and Ted went below and turned in for a two-hour sleep. When they climbed up through the forward hatch again after breakfast it was to find the sun shining bright and the fleet moving majestically eastward.

Chief Gunner's Mate Mike Mowrey confided to them that the Dewey was, indeed, bound for European waters. Lieutenant McClure had opened his sealed orders and learned that he was to report to the Vice-Admiral in the North Sea. Word had been passed around to the ship's officers and they in turn were "tipping off" their men. The Dewey was stripped for action and was to assist the destroyers in defense of the transports in the event of an attack.

The first day out was spent in drills and target practice. Late in the afternoon a huge warship was sighted dead ahead and for a time there was a bit of anxious waiting aboard the Dewey. While it was generally known that the German high seas fleet was bottled up in the Kiel Canal, there was always a chance of running into a stray raider. But very shortly the oncoming vessel broke out a flutter of flags, indicating that she was a French cruiser, and exchanged salutations with the commander of the American fleet.

The men of the Dewey soon learned that the troopships which they were escorting carried a number of regiments of marines and several detachments of U.S. Regulars bound for France. Because the submarines were slower than either the transports or the destroyers, the fleet made slow progress.

They had been at sea over a week and were entering the war zone when, late one afternoon, there came a sharp cry from the lookout in the Dewey's deck steering station.

"Periscope two points off the starboard!"

Instantly an alarm to general quarters was sounded. Jack and Ted, detailed in the same gun crew, had just come on duty at the forward gun. The Dewey's wireless was flashing the news to the rest of the fleet.

The destroyers drew in closer to the troopships and began immediately belching forth dense black clouds of smoke under forced draft that the boys divined instantly as the smoke screens used so effectively as a curtain to blind the eyes of the U-boats.

Turning her nose outward from the hidden transports the Dewey drew away in a wide sweeping circle to starboard.

"All hands below!" came the order. Immediately the deck guns were made fast and the crew scrambled down through the hatches. In a few minutes, driving ahead at full speed, the Dewey was submerged until only her periscopes showed.

All at once the crew heard a shout from the conning tower.

"There she is!" yelled Lieutenant McClure, as he stood with his eyes glued to the periscope glass.

"U-boat driving straight ahead at the smoke curtain. Port the helm!" he commanded.

The Dewey came around sharp and, in response to the guidance of her commander, began to ascend.

Having executed a flank movement, the Dewey now was endeavoring to engineer a surprise attack on the German submarine from the rear. To all intents, the German commander had not yet noted the approaching American submersible. He was going after the transports full tilt, hoping to bore through the destroyers' smoke curtain and torpedo one of the Yankee fleet.

Quickly the Dewey dived up out of the water, the hatches were thrown open and the gun crews swarmed on deck, carrying shells for their guns. Jack and Ted followed Mike Mowrey on deck and dropped into position behind

"Roosey." Gazing ahead they could make out the German periscope and its foamy trail.

"Fire on that periscope," ordered Lieutenant McClure.

The U-boat was not more than nine hundred yards away, according to the Dewey's range-finder, and apparently yet unconscious of the proximity of the American submarine. In a moment the gun was loaded and ready for firing.

"Bang!" she spoke, and then every eye followed the shot. Commander McClure had jumped up on the conning tower and was hugging the periscope pole. There was a moment's silence before he spoke.

"A little short, boys," he called. "Elevate just a little more—-you've nearly got the range."

Again the gun crew leaped into action.

"Hurry, boys! he sees us now and is beginning to submerge!" yelled the young lieutenant as he followed the U-boat through his glasses.

Again "Roosey" spoke, and this time with an emphatic "crack" that boded ill for any luckless human who might get within the line of its screaming shell fire.

"O-o-o-oh, great!" cried Lieutenant McClure an instant later as he peered more intently through his glasses.

Of a sudden the periscope disappeared from the crest of the sea as though wiped out completely by the explosion of the Dewey's shell.

"No doubt of it, boys; you ripped off that periscope," announced

McClure, with an air of finality.

At their commander's words the gun crew burst into cheers. The submersible's wireless was singing out a message of good cheer to the American fleet. It was only too evident that the enemy U-boat had been crippled and put completely to rout by the daring maneuvers and deadly gunfire of the Dewey.

"Who said the Yanks couldn't stop their pesky undersea wasps?" chattered Bill Witt joyously. "If they just let us loose long enough we'll show 'em how to kill poison with poison."

Mike Mowrey was in great glee.

"Just like a grasshopper begging for mercy on a bass hook," he said jauntily, imitating with a crook of his finger the disappearing periscope.

Soon the fleet was off Cape Clear on the southernmost point of the Irish coast and very shortly headed well into the English Channel. Now every few hours the American warships were speaking one or other of the English and French patrol ships. Great was the joy of the boys aboard the Dewey when first they beheld an American destroyer out on the firing line.

"Union Jack and French tricolor look pretty good; but none of them makes a fellow's blood tingle like the Stars and Stripes; eh, chum?" queried Jack, as he surveyed an American destroyer dashing along in fine fettle. And Ted heartily agreed.

Off Falmouth, the transports, accompanied by three of the American destroyers and two English "limeys "—-as the British destroyers are known in the slang of the sea—-slipped off silently into the twilight. The American infantry and marines were to be landed "somewhere in France." Jack and Ted viewed the departure with mingled pride and regret.

"Reckon they will be in the trenches before long," ventured Ted.

"Frisking bean balls at the Fritzes," snapped Bill Witt with a chuckle as he joined his mates.

And now the submarine fleet continued on its way into the North Sea. An American destroyer, two English "limeys" and a French vessel of the same type were to escort the Yankee subs the rest of the way. By morning the Dewey had slipped through the Strait of Dover and emerged at last into the North Sea—-the field of her future activities!

There, in due time, the subs reported to the American admiral. Without any delay they were detailed for duty in the vast arena stretching down the Strait of Dover northward to the Norwegian coast—-from Wilhelmshaven to the east coast of England and Scotland.

Provisioned and refueled after an inspection and test of her engines, the Dewey lost no time in getting out on the firing line. London papers, brought on board while the Yankee submersible rested in the English naval station at Chatham, told of a daring raid by German light cruisers on the east coast of England only the night before. Eluding the allied patrol ships, the raiders had slipped through the entente lines and bombarded a number of coast towns, escaping finally in a running fight with English cruisers.

"That was before we got over here," said Bill Witt with a show of irony as he read the meager dispatch in the London Times. "Wait till we Yanks meet up with the Huns!"

An opportunity came shortly. One night, little more than a week after the Dewey had put out into the North Sea, she ran plumb into a huge warship.

The little submarine had taken a position about twenty miles directly west of the great German stronghold at Heligoland in a lane likely to be traveled by any outcoming warships.

Executive Officer Cleary, alone in the conning tower, had suddenly been apprised of the approach of the vessel by a message from the wireless room. The Dewey was floating in twenty feet of water with only her periscopes, protruding above the surface. Hardly had he gazed into the glass before he made out dimly the outlines of the approaching vessel.

At once the crew was sounded to quarters.

"German raider!" the muffled cry ran through the ship.

CHAPTER V

THE GERMAN RAIDERS

As the Dewey settled into the water. Lieutenant McClure and his executive officer peered intently though the periscopes, hoping to catch sight of the unknown craft and speculating on her nationality. The sky was flecked with clouds and there was no convenient moon to aid the submarine sentinel—-an ideal night for a raid! "Little Mack," as the crew had affectionately named their commander, was in a quandary as to whether the approaching vessel was friend or foe.

"We'll lie right here and watch him awhile," he told his executive officer. "Pretty soon he'll be close enough for us to get a line on his silhouette."

It had been an interesting revelation to the Brighton boys soon after their entry into the navy to learn that each ship was equipped with a silhouette book. By means of this it was possible to tell the vessels of one nation from another by the size and formation of their hulls, their smokestacks and general outline. Each officer had to be thoroughly well informed on the contents of the book.

Quietly, stealthily the hidden submarine awaited the approach of her adversary, for it seemed only too certain that the ship that had suddenly come dashing up out of the east was out of Cuxhaven or Wilhelmshaven, and had but a short time before passed under the mighty German guns on Heligoland.

Chief Gunner Mowrey and his crew in the torpedo chamber forward were signaled to "stand by the guns ready for action," which meant in this case the huge firing tubes and the Whitehead torpedoes. Jack and Ted fell into their places, stripped to the waist, and making sure that the reserve torpedoes were ready for any emergency.

By adjusting the headpiece of the ship's microphone to his ears Chief Electrician Sammy Smith kept close tabs on the approaching vessel with the underwater telephone. With the receivers to his hears he could hear plainly the swish of the vessel's propeller blades as she bore down upon the floating submarine. With his reports as a basis for their deductions, the Dewey's officers were able to figure out the position of the mystery ship and to tell accurately the distance between the two vessels.

"Reckon he'll be dead off our bow in a minute or so," observed Cleary as he completed another observation based on Smith's latest report.

McClure sprang again to the periscope.

"Yes, we ought to get a line on him soon enough now," was his rejoinder.

For a moment the two officers studied the haze of the night sea around them, unable yet to discern the form of the approaching vessel. And then came a huge specter, looming up directly off the starboard quarter of the Dewey in the proportions of a massive warship.

"Looks like a German cruiser," said the American lieutenant as he gripped the brass wheel of the periscope and gave himself intently to the task of divining the identity of the unknown ship.

Cleary was making observations at the reserve periscope, the two officers having plunged the conning tower of the Dewey in utter darkness that they might better observe the shadowy hulk bearing down upon them.

"It is a German cruiser—-Plauen class—-and coming up in a hurry at better than twenty knots," exclaimed McClure, as the outline of the ship was implanted clean-cut against the horizon dead ahead of the Dewey.

His hand on the firing valve, the submarine commander waited only until the bow of the German warship showed on the range glass of the periscope, and then released a torpedo.

Instantly a great volume of compressed air swirled into the upper port chamber; the bowcap was opened and the missile sped on its way.

"Gee, I hope that 'moldy' lands her!" shouted Jack at the sound of the discharged torpedo.

Although but a short time in the North Sea and just getting well acquainted with their English cousins, the American lads were fast learning the lingo of the deep. To every man aboard the Dewey a torpedo was a "moldy," so named by the English seamen.

As the torpedo crew sprang to reload the emptied chamber the Dewey's diving rudders were turned, ballast was shipped and she started to dive. The plunge came none too soon. A lookout on the German cruiser, eagle-eyed about his daring venture, had noted the approaching torpedo and sounded an alarm. At the same moment the ship's rudder was thrown over and she swung to starboard, paralleling the position of the Dewey. And just as she came around one of her big searchlights aft flashed into life and shot its bright rays over the water. For a moment or two a finger of ghostly white shifted aimlessly to and fro over the surf ace of the sea and then centered full upon the disappearing periscope of the Dewey! Instantly came the boom of the ship's guns as they belched a salvo at the tormenting submarine.

"Missed him by inches," growled McClure after waiting long enough to be convinced that the torpedo had sped wide of the mark.

"And he is firing with all his aft guns," added Cleary as he observed further the flashes of fire from the turrets of the German cruiser.

McClure signaled for the Dewey to be submerged with all speed.

"He'll never get us," he announced a few seconds later as the submarine dived down out of sight.

Jack and Ted, with the rest of their crew, had by this time shunted another Whitehead into position, adjusted the mechanism and were standing by awaiting developments.

"Just our luck to slip a moldy to the blooming Boche and draw a blank," grumbled Mike Mowrey, who was mad as a hornet over the "miss."

Ted was inclined to be a bit pessimistic, too; but Jack was sure the Dewey would make good on her next try. Bill Witt started to sing: "We'll hang Kaiser Bill to a sour apple tree," but got little response. The torpedo crew were glum over their failure to bag the German raiding cruiser and in no mood for singing.

"Cheer up, boys; better luck next time," called out Navigating Officer

Binns as he peered into the torpedo compartment.

All at once the boys were startled by a cry from Sammy Smith, who had suddenly leaped to his feet and stood swaying in the wireless room with both microphone receivers tightly pressed to his ears. Above the clatter of the Dewey's engines the gunners forward could hear the electrician talking excitedly to Lieutenant McClure.

"Listen, listen, other ships are coming up," Smith was shouting. "I can hear their propellers. That's the fellow we missed moving off there on our port quarter. You can hear at least two more here in the starboard microphone. We seem to have landed plumb in the nest of a German raiding party," rattled off the electrician glibly as he passed the receivers to his commander for a verification of his report.

McClure snatched the apparatus and clamped it to his ears. For a moment he listened to the mechanical whirr of churning propellers, borne into his senses through the submarine telephone.

"Great!" he exclaimed. "Some more of the Kaiser's vaunted navy trying to sneak away from their home base for a bit of trickery."

As he rang the engine room to shut off power, the American commander added, with flashing eyes:

"If we don't bring down one of these prowlers before this night is over

I'll go back home and ship as deckhand on a Jersey City ferry-boat."

Suspended fifty feet below the surface of the sea, the Dewey floated like a cork in a huge basin while her officers took further observations on the movements of the German warships above them. Now that their presence was known the American officers realized they would be accorded a stiff reception when they next went "up top.".

"I'm going to try it," announced McClure shortly. "We'll take a chance and pay our respects to one of their tubs."

The Dewey forthwith began to rise. At the direction of the navigating officer two hundred pounds of ballast were expelled. Tilting fore and aft like a rocking horse, the submersible responded gradually to the lightening process until at last the depth dial showed only a margin of several feet needed to lift the eyes of the periscopes above the waves. The little steel-encased clock in the conning tower showed ten minutes past one—-just about the right time for a night raiding party to be getting under way.

"Guess we'll lie here and wait for them to come along," whispered McClure to Cleary as the periscopes popped up out of the depths into the night gloom.

"We seem to be right in their path and may be able to get one of them as he shoots across our bow," added Cleary as he took another telephone report from the wireless room.

According to Sammy Smith's observations there were two vessels coming up to starboard, while the third, the one the Dewey had missed, was dim in the port microphone and almost out of range. Engines shut off, the submarine lay entirely concealed, awaiting the coming of her prey. It was McClure's idea to lie perfectly still in the water until one of the enemy warships swung right into the range glass of the Dewey and then give it a stab of steel—-a sting in the dark from a hidden serpent!

The waiting moments seemed like hours. Gradually, however, the leader of the silent ships drew nearer. There was no mistaking the telltale reports in the wireless room. Basing his calculations on the chief electrician's reports, McClure figured the leader of the oncoming squadron to be now not more than half a mile away and moving steadily forward toward the desired range—-a dead line on the bow of the Dewey.

Executive Officer Cleary at the reserve periscope was first to detect the mass of steel looming up out of the darkness. Lieutenant McClure swung his periscope several degrees to starboard and drew a bead on the German warship an instant later.

"We'll drop this chap just as he shoots across our bow," declared the Dewey's commander.

Five hundred yards away came the speeding warship. It was close enough now for the American officers to make out her outlines in detail and to satisfy themselves that this was another member of the raiding party out of the great German naval base in back of Heligoland.

"All right, here goes," shouted the doughty Yankee skipper a moment later as the German cruiser drew up until her bow edged into the circle that McClure had marked off on the periscope as the exact spot on which to aim his fire.

Swish! went the torpedo as it shot from the bow of the Dewey and straightened out in the water on its foamy trail, cutting through the sea like a huge swordfish.

It took only a moment—-an interval of time during which the torpedo from the American submarine and the German cruiser seemed irresistibly drawn toward each other. And then came the crash—-the impact of the torpedo's war-nose against the steel side of the cruiser, the detonation of the powerful explosive, the rending of the German hull.

And then, loud enough for his crew forward to hear his words, McClure called out:

"A perfect hit, boys; torpedo landed plumb in the engine room of a big

German cruiser."

A great cheer resounded through the hull of the American undersea craft as the good news was borne to the torpedo crew forward and to the engine room aft.

Keeping his eyes to the periscope, McClure beheld the most spectacular picture that had yet been glimpsed through the eye of the American submarine. The torpedo had struck squarely abaft the ship's magazine and wrecked her completely. The night was painted a lurid glow as a titanic explosion shook the sea and a mass of yellow flame completely enveloped the doomed warship from stem to stern.

"Look, she is going down by the stern," called out Officer Cleary as he took one last squint at the Dewey's quarry just before the stricken warship slipped away into the depths.

The jubilation of the crew knew no bounds. The men were wild with joy over their success. Jack and Chief Gunner Mowrey were "mitting" each other like a prize fighter and his manager after a big fight, while Ted and Bill Witt were clawing each other like a pair of wild men.

Through the main periscope Commander McClure was noting the death struggle of the German cruiser, when Executive Officer Cleary, swinging the reserve periscope around to scan the horizon aft the Dewey, suddenly called out sharply:

"Submerge, quick! Right here abaft our conning tower to starboard comes a destroyer. She is aimed directly at us and almost on top of us. Hurry, or we are going to be run down!"

CHAPTER VI

RAMMED BY A DESTROYER

It was a critical moment aboard the American submarine. Out of the darkness the destroyer—-speed king of the modern navies—-had emerged just at the moment the Dewey was sending home the shot that laid low the German cruiser.

Dashing along at a speed better than thirty knots an hour, the greyhound of the Teutonic fleet was bearing down hard upon the Yankee. Evidently the lookout on the destroyer had marked the path of the Dewey's torpedo in the dim gray of the night sea, and with his skipper had sent his craft charging full tilt at the American "wasp."

"If they get to us before we submerge we are done for," gasped Lieutenant McClure, as he bellowed orders to Navigating Officer Binns to lower away as fast as the submerging apparatus would permit. Then the quick-witted commander rang the engine room full speed ahead at the same time he threw the helm hard to port in an effort to bring his craft around parallel with the charging destroyer and thus make a smaller target.

Down, down, down sank the Dewey as her valves were opened and the sea surged into the ballast tanks. The periscopes had been well out of water when the destroyer had first been sighted. It was now a race between two cool and cunning naval officers—-the German to hurl his vessel full upon the American submarine and deal it a death blow; the American skipper to outwit and outmaneuver his antagonist by putting the Dewey down where she would be safe from the steel nose of the destroyer.

Although no word was spoken to the crew, they could sense the situation by the sharp commands emanating from the conning tower and the celerity with which the navigating officer and his assistant were working the ballast pumps.

Great beads of perspiration stood out on the forehead of Officer Binns as he stood over the array of levers and gave directions, first to ship ballast in one tank, and then in another, shifting the added weight evenly so as not to disturb the equilibrium of the Dewey and cause her to go hurtling to the bottom, top heavy in either bow or stern.

Nearly two minutes were necessary to get the little undersea craft down far enough to evade the prow of the oncoming destroyer, and even then the conning tower furnished a target that might be crushed by the nose of the enemy ship and precipitate an avalanche of water into the hold—-with disaster for the men assembled at their posts of duty.

"They are right on top of us now," screamed Sammy Smith as he hugged the microphone receivers to his ears.

If the destroyer was going to get the submarine, now was the fatal moment!

The Dewey suddenly lunged like a great tiger leaping from the limb of a tree upon its prey. Responding to a signal from his commander, Chief Engineer Blaine had suddenly shot into the submarine's engines the full power of the electric storage batteries and hurled the Dewey forward with a great burst of speed. There was a slim chance that the swift-moving German warship might be sidestepped by a quick maneuver, and the crafty McClure was leaving no deep-sea trick unturned.

"Nice place for the Fritzes to swing overboard one of those infernal depth bombs," muttered Bill Witt.

A depth bomb! Jack and Ted knew all about the latest device being employed by the warring nations in their campaigns against submarines. Gigantic grenades, they were, carrying deadly and powerful explosives timed to go off at any desired depth. One of them dropped from the deck of the destroyer as it passed over the spot where the Dewey had submerged might blow the diminutive ship to atoms.

With reckless abandon big bluff Bill Witt began to sing:

"It's a long way to Tipperary, It's a long way to go. It's a long way—-"

The song was interrupted by a harsh grating sound—-the crashing of steel against steel—-and then the Dewey shuddered from stem to stern as though it had run suddenly against a stone wall.

Hurled from his feet by the fearful impact Jack sprawled on the steel floor of the torpedo room. Ted, standing close by his chum, clutched at one of the reserve torpedoes hanging in the rack in time to prevent himself falling.

For a moment the Dewey appeared to be going down by the stern, with her bow inclined upward at an angle of forty-five degrees. Above all the din and confusion could be heard the roar of a terrific explosion outside. The little submersible was caught in the convulsion of the sea until it seemed her seams would be rent and her crew engulfed.

From the engine room Chief Engineer Blaine and his men retreated amidships declaring that the submarine had been dealt a powerful blow directly aft the conning tower on her starboard beam.

"Any plates leaking?" asked Lieutenant McClure quietly.

"Not that we can notice, sir," replied Blame. "It appears as though the nose of that Prussian scraped along our deck line abaft the conning tower."

At any moment the steel plates were likely to cave in under the strain and the submarine be inundated.

"Stand by ready for the emergency valve!" shouted Lieutenant McClure.

This was the ship's safety contrivance. The Brighton boys had been wonderfully impressed with it shortly after their first introduction to the "innards" of a submarine.

The safety valve could be set for any desired depth; when the vessel dropped to that depth the ballast tanks were automatically opened and every ounce of water expelled. As a result the submarine would shoot to the surface. The older "submarine salts" called the safety the "tripper."

"If they've punctured us we might as well cut loose and take our chances on the surface," declared Lieutenant McClure to the little group of officers standing with him amidships in the control chamber.

Not a man dissented. They were content to abide by the word of their chieftain. It was some relief to know that the nose of the destroyer had not crashed through the skin of the submarine; but, from the concussion astern and Chief Engineer Blaine's report, it was very evident that the Dewey had been struck a glancing blow. Deep-sea pressure against a weakened plate could have but one inevitable sequel—-the rending of the ship's hull.

"They have gone completely over us," came the announcement from the wireless room.

Hardly had the electrician concluded the report before the Dewey was rocked by another submarine detonation—-the explosion of a second depth bomb. This time it was farther from the hiding vessel; however, the ship was shaken until every electric light blinked in its socket.

"I hope they soon get done with their Fourth of July celebration," remarked Bill Witt by way of a bit of subsea repartee.

"That's the way they blow holes in their schweitzer cheese," ventured

Mike Mowrey with a chuckle.

It was decided to submerge a little deeper and then leisurely inspect the interior hull aft. An observation with the microphones disclosed the fact that the destroyer was moving out into the North Sea.

"Guess they think they got us that time," suggested Lieutenant McClure to his executive officer.

"Was rather a close call, come to think of it," smiled Cleary.

The latter went aft with Chief Engineer Blaine for the hull inspection and returned in a few moments to say that, so far as could be observed from the interior, she had not been dealt a severe blow. The executive officer ventured the opinion that the keel of the destroyer had brushed along the aft deck, thus accounting for the fact that the submarine had suddenly been tilted downward at the stern.

"We'll not dare submerge too deep," said Lieutenant McClure. "Pressure against our hull increases, you know, at the rate of four and a quarter pounds to the square inch for every ten feet we submerge. It may be our plates were weakened by that collision. We'll go down to one hundred feet and lie there until these ships get out of the way."

The depth dial showed eighty feet. More water, accordingly, was shipped and the Dewey slipped away to the desired depth, when the intake of ballast ceased and the tiny vessel floated alone in the sea. Determined to take no more chances with the Kaiser's navy until he had ascertained the true condition of his own vessel, Lieutenant McClure decided to lie-to here in safety.

When the raiders had departed he would ascend and make a more detailed external inspection of the hull.

It was half-past two. Jean Cartier superintended the distribution of hot coffee and light "chow" and the crew made themselves comfortable in their submarine home.

Half an hour later, when it had been determined by the telephones that the German ships had moved on westward, the Dewey began again to ascend the depths.

Early dawn was streaking the sky with tints of orange gray when at last the submarine poked its periscopes above the waves. Not a ship was in sight; there was not a trace of the battle cruiser that the Dewey had sent to her doom during the earlier hours of the night.

"Didn't have a chance, did they?" Ted said to his churn in contemplation of the fate of the German warship.

Jack felt different about it.

"Sure they had a chance," he answered.

"They would have gotten us if we hadn't landed them first."

"Do the other fellow as you know he would do you," Jack philosophized.

As the Dewey emerged again on the surface with her deck and super-structure exposed, the ship's wireless aerials were run up and she prepared to get in touch with the United States fleet. Jack crept into the wireless room that he might better understand what was going on. Lately he had been learning the wireless code and familiarizing himself with the operation of the radio under the kindly instruction of Sammy Smith.

"You never know when knowledge of these things is going to stand you in good stead," remarked Jack when he had applied to Sammy for "a bit in electricity."

Once more the hatches were opened and the crew swarmed out to stretch their limbs and get a breath of fresh air again. Lieutenant McClure hastened to examine the deck of the Dewey to ascertain whether any damage had been done in the collision with the destroyer.

Yes, there was a slight dent—-a broad scar—-running obliquely across the deck plates just aft the conning tower within a few inches of the engine room hatch. The damage, however, appeared to be slight.

"Narrow escape," the lieutenant pondered.

"Zip! zip!" the wireless was sputtering as Sammy Smith flung a code message into space in quest of other members of the allied navies. Several times he shot out the call and then closed his key to await a reply.

Finally it came—-a radio from an American warship far out of sight over the horizon.

"Take this radio to Lieutenant McClure," said Sammy, as he typed it with the wireless receiver still to his ears, and wheeled to hand it to Jack. The latter took the flimsy sheet and bounded up the aft hatch to where his commander stood examining the hull.

"American and English cruisers and destroyers in running fight with German raiding squadron. Give us your position. U.S.S. Salem," the message ran.

At once the Dewey's latitude and longitude were rattled off to the Salem. In reply came another radio from the scout cruiser, giving the position of the raiding fleet and the pursuers, with this direction:

"Close in from your position. German fleet in full retreat headed

E.N.E. across North Sea. You may be able to intercept them!"

CHAPTER VII

IN A MINE FIELD

Without any further ado the Dewey got under way. While the inspection of the hull had been going on the submarine's batteries had been recharged and she was ready again for further diving upon a moment's notice. Lieutenant McClure climbed into the deck steering station—-the bridge of a submarine—-and assumed charge of the electric rudder control, the wheel of a submersible.

Jack and Ted were ordered onto the bridge with their commander and instructed to keep a sharp lookout on the horizon with powerful glasses. The wireless was snapping away exchanging messages with the allied fleet and getting a line on the pursued raiders. The cool fresh air felt invigorating after the night's cramped vigil in the fetid air of the submarine.

When mess call sounded, Jack and Ted, relieved from duty, went below to get some "chow" and snatch an hour or two of rest.

A radiogram was handed Lieutenant McClure while at breakfast giving the position of the U.S.S. Chicago. A little later H.M.S. Congo, a "limey," was spoken. Soon the sub was hearing the chatter of half a dozen American and English warships.

Hastening back to the conning tower, Lieutenant McClure conferred for a few moments with his executive officer and as a result of their calculations the course of the Dewey was altered. Headed due north, it was the aim of the submarine officers to intercept the retreating column of German raiders whom they knew now to be in full retreat, hotly pursued by the allied squadron.

Not half an hour had elapsed when the lookout reported a blur on the horizon that, despite the mist of early morning, was easily discernible as the smoke of several vessels under forced draft. Very soon the head of the column loomed over the horizon—-a German cruiser in the lead—-followed closely by a destroyer that was belching forth dense black smoke from its funnels.

"They are making for home under a smoke screen from their destroyers, and I'll bet some of our ships are not very far away either," was Lieutenant McClure's observation as he stood surveying the field of action through his glass.

"Yes, and that destroyer there is probably the chap who nearly ran us down last night," added Executive Officer Cleary.

Lieutenant McClure nodded assent and then turned toward Jack, who had been watching the approaching Germans from a position on deck just aft the conning tower.

The Dewey's commander motioned the young seaman to climb into the steering station.

"I want you to stand right by and act as my aide," said McClure.

"That goes, not only now, but until further orders. You and Mr.

Wainwright will relieve each other as my aides. Go below and tell

Chief Engineer Blaine we are about to close in on the Huns and want

all the speed possible during the next hour or so."

Jack saluted and lowered away into the conning tower hatch. As he climbed down into the hull he heard the sound of heavy cannonading across the water. It was certain now that a running fight was in progress and that behind the veil of the black German destroyer smoke were allied warships.

The retreating column was well off the port bow and racing eastward toward the shelter of the big guns at Heligoland. Coming up out of the south the American submarine had run at right angles into the line of the Hun retreat. The Dewey held a strategic position. She viewed the approaching squadron as though looking down the hypotenuse of the angle. The Germans were speeding along the base. The Dewey had but to slip down the perpendicular to intercept the panicky Prussians.

And that was just what Lieutenant McClure proposed doing. All hands were ordered below and the hatches sealed. Running on the surface, the oil engines were put to their best endeavor and the Dewey cleft the whitecaps at her best speed.

"Go forward, Mr. Hammond, and inquire of Chief Gunner Mowrey how many torpedoes we have aboard," ordered Lieutenant McClure.

Jack hurried away and returned in a few minutes to report that all four tubes were loaded and two auxiliary Whiteheads in the racks. The Dewey's torpedo range was two miles, but her commander preferred to be within less than six hundred yards for a sure shot.

McClure could now see the leader of the German squadron—-a powerful battle cruiser—-crowding on all speed. His guns astern, powerful fourteen-inch pieces in twin turrets, were in action, firing huge salvos at his pursuers. The destroyer rode far to starboard of the cruiser, emitting a steady stream of smoke designed to blind the eyes of the pursuers.

Jockeying into position after another twenty minutes' run, the Dewey's commander decided to let loose with a torpedo. The cruiser had pulled up now until it was nearly dead ahead of the American submersible. The destroyer was dancing along several hundreds yards in the rear of the cruiser.

So intent were the Germans on keeping away from the pursuing warships that they had not noticed the sly little submarine that had slipped up out of the south!

Jack had now an opportunity to witness the actual firing of a torpedo at an enemy vessel at close range. Directly in front of the Dewey's commander, just above the electric rudder button, glowed four little light bulbs in bright red—-one for each of the torpedo tubes in the bow bulkhead. When they were lighted thus it indicated that every chamber was loaded. As soon as a torpedo was discharged the bulb corresponding with the empty tube faded out. Lieutenant McClure had but to touch the electric contact under each bulb to send one of the death-dealing torpedoes on its way. This Jack was to see in a moment.

Crouching with his eyes to the periscope until the racing German cruiser drew up to the desired fret on the measured glass McClure clutched the lower port toggle and released a torpedo. Again the jarring motion that indicated the discharge of the missile and the swirl of the compressed air forward. Through the eye of the forward periscope the commander of the Dewey followed the course of the torpedo as it skimmed away from his bow.

"There she goes!" exclaimed Executive Officer Cleary as the mirror reflected the frothing wake of the giant Whitehead.

For a moment or so there was a breathless silence in the conning tower of the Yankee sub as the two officers followed their shot. Only for a moment however, for Commander McClure, knowing full well the German destroyer would sight the speeding torpedo and immediately turn its fire on the Yankee's periscopes, gave orders to submerge. But as the Dewey lowered away he gazed ahead once more. The spectacle that greeted him made the blood leap fast in his veins.

"It's a hit!" he yelled in sheer delight.

So it proved. Officer Cleary, still straining at the reserve periscope, beheld the same picture. The torpedo had shot across the bow of the destroyer and leaped forward to finally bury its steel nose in the great gray side of the cruiser.

"Almost directly amidships," called out "Little Mack."

And then, as the Dewey plunged beneath the waves, Lieutenant McClure explained eagerly how he had beheld the explosion of the torpedo just aft the main forward battery turret directly on the line of the forward smoke funnel.

"Giving them a dose of their own medicine," ejaculated Cleary as his commander turned laughingly from the periscope.

"This will settle a few scores for the Lusitania, to say nothing of the many more ships with defenseless men and women that have been sunk since the beginning of the war," added McClure seriously. Then turning to Jack Hammond he added: "I guess you are the good-luck chap. We got both those Boche boats since I called you into the turret as my aide. Don't forget, you are to stay right here permanently."

Jack saluted mechanically, but his heart beat high and he could scarce repress an exclamation of delight.

At a depth of sixty feet the Dewey's engines were slowed down and she floated gracefully out of range of the German destroyer. After traveling ahead for half a mile the submersible was stopped again and began slowly to ascend.

As the eye of the periscope projected again out of the sea Lieutenant

McClure hastened to get a glimpse of his surroundings.

There, off the port bow, lay the crippled German cruiser—-the same vessel that had been hit by the Dewey's torpedo. She was listing badly from the effect of the American submarine's unexpected sting and had turned far over on her side. A British destroyer was standing by rescuing members of the Teuton crew as they flung themselves into the water from their overturning craft.

Far off the Dewey's starboard bow could be seen a moving column of warships—-the remnants of the German raiding fleet in the van, followed by the English and American patrol vessels.

"Useless for us to follow them," declared McClure, as he took in the situation. "Might as well stand by this stricken Hun cruiser and pick up some of her floating crew."

"There's a lot of them in the water," said Cleary, as he swung the other periscope to scan the open sea well to the sinking cruiser's stern.

In a few minutes the Dewey ascended and made herself known to the

British "limey." Over the decks of the latter clambered several score

German seamen who had been fished from a watery grave.

A stiff wind had come up out of the southeast and was kicking the sea into rollers with whitecaps. However, the men of the Dewey, armed with life preservers, steadied themselves on the turtle-back deck of their craft, and started the hunt for swimming Germans.

Ted had joined Jack forward, carrying a coil of rope, and they were scanning the sea, when their attention was diverted by the gesticulations of Bill Witt standing well forward. He was pointing off to port.

"Look—-a floating mine!" he shouted. Almost at the same moment Jack spied another mine closer up off the starboard quarter.

In a mine field! The retreating German warships had strewn the sea with the deadly implements of naval warfare, and the Dewey had come up almost on top of a number of the unanchored explosives!

CHAPTER VIII

A RESCUE

"If one of them pill boxes bumps us on the water line it's all day with your Uncle Sam's U-boat Dewey," vouchsafed Bill Witt as he stood surveying the mine field into which they had stumbled.

In response to the warning from the lookout forward, Lieutenant McClure had stopped the submarine and was taking account of the dangers that beset his ship. The sea was running high and it was hard to discern the mines except when they were carried up on the swell of the waves.

Swept along thus with the rise and fall of water, one of the floating missiles seemed now bearing down upon the Dewey's port bow. Lieutenant McClure saw it just as a huge wave picked up the whirling bomb and carried it closer up toward the submarine.

"All hands below; ready to submerge!" he called out sharply, at the same time directing Executive Officer Cleary to get the Dewey under way.

"Stay here with me a moment," continued McClure, addressing Jack. They were standing alone on the forward deck.

Another wave brought the mine dangerously close.

"You armed?" called out Lieutenant McClure.

"Yes, sir," replied Jack, as he drew his heavy navy automatic.

"Shoot at that mine, boy," commanded the officer. At the same time the young lieutenant drew his own weapon and began blazing away. He hoped thus to explode the deadly thing before it was hurled against the Dewey.

Jack followed suit. The target, however, was so buffeted about by the waves that it was next to impossible to sight on it. The only thing to do was to fire at random, hoping against hope that a lucky shot would result in the detonation of the mine.

"It's no use," shouted McClure above the crack of the firearms and the roar of the sea.

Their shots were rattling harmlessly off the metallic sides of the mine.

By now Cleary had swung the Dewey around until she was pointed almost directly at the nearest mine, it being slightly off the port quarter. The engines had been reversed and started, and the submarine was drawing away.

"We ought to clear this one and then be able to dive and get out of here," said McClure.

But as he spoke a huge wave lifted the mine again and flung it full in the path of the submarine. As though drawn by some mysterious magnet the floating explosive seemed following the Dewey at every turn—-an unrelenting nemesis bent on the destruction of the American vessel.

"Quick, Jack; grab that wireless upright forward!" commanded the young lieutenant.

With alacrity Jack flung himself upon the steel aerial and wrenched it loose. It was a long tubing very much like an ordinary length of gas pipe set up usually forward as one of the wireless supports, and folding down into the deck plates when the Dewey was stripped for undersea navigation.

"I am going to take a chance on exploding that one mine that seems to be our hoodoo," shouted Lieutenant McClure.

Jack waited anxiously to see just what his lieutenant was doing. Taking the wireless upright in hand after the manner of a track athlete throwing the javelin, the young commander drew it well back and then launched it full upon the mine floating not more than fifteen or twenty feet from the Dewey.

"Hit it!" exclaimed McClure as the improvised battering ram left his strong right arm.

It did, and with the desired result. The impact of the long steel tubing directly upon the shell of the mine was sufficient to explode the deadly thing. A terrific detonation rent the air and immediately a column of water was hurled high, towering over the Dewey like a geyser, and then engulfing the little submarine. Jack and his commander were swept off their feet in the deluge. As though some unseen hand had suddenly clutched them with a grip of steel the pair were flung from the deck of their craft into the seething foam.

It seemed an endless eternity to Jack as he was carried down into the depths. The roar of a million cataracts throbbed in his brain and before his mind flashed the panorama of his life. Home—-Winchester—-Brighton—-all the old chums and the "profs!"

Death seemed so near to the youth as ho felt his strength giving way. His senses reeled. In his ears pealed the medley of a thousand bells. In this horrible abyss he knew he could not long survive.

Then, just when it seemed life was gone, his head shot up out of the water and he found himself swimming free and breathing normally again. Above, the same old blue sky. Turning over on his back and paddling thus until he floated, the boy remembered gain the submersible and the fearful mine explosion that had cast him into the sea.

He looked for the Dewey and in a moment beheld it still riding the waves. Yes, the old sub had survived the mine explosion, or at least, was still afloat, if damaged.

But what about Lieutenant McClure? Now Jack recalled his gallant commander and how he, too, had been cast from the deck in the deluge. Was "Little Mack" still alive?

The Dewey was slowly picking her way among the other mines. Jack shouted to her, but getting no response he started to swim with vigorous strokes. He had gone but a few yards when an object appeared on the crest of the water directly in front of him. It took only a glance to convince him that it was the form of Lieutenant McClure. With a supreme effort Jack drove himself forward with mighty strokes toward the inert form of his commander.

Glancing up for a moment, what was the delight of the youth battling with death to see the Dewey bearing down upon him!

Some one had seen him and they were coming to his rescue.

The sight renewed his strength. After what seemed a long while Jack was able to clutch the collar of his chief officer. "Little Mack" was unconscious.

By degrees Jack succeeded in turning over the limp form until it floated face upward. Locking his left arm securely around the neck of the apparently lifeless officer so that the face was held above the surface of the water, and using his strong right arm and legs, Jack began swimming as best he could in the general direction of the submarine that he knew to be not far away.

The weight of the lieutenant's body dragged heavily upon his left arm. His strength was ebbing away fast. His arm became numb and his senses chaotic.

Instinctively the lad closed his eyes. It seemed he must let loose the burden tugging in his arms and himself slip away into the depths and into that long sweet sleep that seemed just now so alluring, so compelling.

"Catch the rope when I fling it"—-the words were borne into his stifled senses. It sounded like the voice of his good chum.

Was it Ted? Again came the call, seemingly closer at hand. It was Ted, now faintly, now more clearly. The sound of that voice galvanized the youth in the water.

Jack flung out his free limbs in a frenzy of muscular energy. Something loomed up in the blue of the sky near him and he beheld for one instant the periscopes of the Dewey.

She was drawing closer to the pair in the water!

On the deck stood a number of the crew disregarding the floating mines that had been engaging their attention. Someone was whirling a rope, aiming to throw it to the pair in the water. Every one seemed to be yelling at the same time.

"Hold on—-we are coming—-don't let go—-catch the rope!" Jack heard the calls from his shipmates.

Out over the water spun a coil of rope—-only to fall short of the desired mark and trail off into the sea many yards from the floating pair. Yes, it was Ted, winding frantically again, and yelling encouragement to his chum.

"Hold 'em!" Ted shouted over and over again, just as the Brighton lads had been wont to yell in unison at their football games when the opposing eleven was smashing its way toward Brighton's goal. Once again the coil was ready; once again it was flung outward from the deck of the Dewey. This time it fairly lashed Jack's face. The sting of the hemp seethed to whip new courage into him. Making one last frantic effort he clutched and held the precious rope, just as Ted sprang from the submarine and dived to the rescue.

Jack remembered no more. When he came to he was stretched in his bunk in the hold of the Dewey. Ted was bending over him.

"Thank God you are alive, Jack, old chum!" Ted was murmuring, with glad tears brimming from his eyes.

Jack strove to raise himself on one elbow but fell back limply, weak from the terrible struggle through which he had passed.

"How about 'Little Mack'?" he managed finally to ask faintly.

"Alive but yet unconscious," replied Ted, "They have gotten most of the water out of his lungs and are using the pulmotor."

Jack closed his eyes again and murmured a prayer of thanks for his safe deliverance and for the life of his lieutenant.

"Was the Dewey damaged by the mine explosion?" he asked.

Ted replied that so far as could be determined no serious damage had been inflicted, although Officer Cleary had expressed some apprehension as to the condition of the port seams forward on the under side of the hull. The examination was still in progress.

For an hour Jack rested quietly in his bunk. The Dewey had submerged after taking aboard the half-drowned commander and his rescuer, and at a safe depth gotten safely out of the zone of danger. Now she had come to the surface again for further examination of her hull.

Jack and Ted were conversing in low tones, when Bill Witt stumbled along the passageway leading into the men's quarters and stopped beside Jack. His face was stern.

"What's the matter, Bill—-you seasick?" queried Ted.

"Wish that's all it was," muttered Bill.

"Tell us, what's up?" pressed Ted.

"Isn't very cheery news for a fellow knocked out like Jack after making such a plucky fight for his life and saving his lieutenant," answered Bill with a shrug of his broad shoulders.

Jack smiled.

"If I survived that, I guess I can hear what's troubling you," was his reply.

"Well, it's bad news, boys—-mighty bad," went on Bill. "Chief

Engineer Blaine reports a leak in the main oil reservoir to starboard.

That mine explosion loosened up the seams and the fuel stuff is slowly

but steadily streaming into the deep blue sea!"

CHAPTER IX

VIVE LA FRANCE!

Ted ran aft to the engine room to get a fuller report on the new danger that confronted the Dewey. There he found that what Bill Witt had said was only too true. Either portions of the flying steel from the exploded mine had punctured the skin of the submarine, or else the plates had been loosened by the detonation. The oil was leaking away at an alarming rate and there was no way here in the open sea to get at the leak. The Dewey would have to go into drydock before the repairs could be made.

"But we can navigate with our batteries, can't we?" Ted inquired of Sammy Smith, who had come out of the wireless room to better acquaint himself with the Dewey's newest tale of woe.

Sammy was not at all comforting.

"I understand the batteries, are pretty well exhausted," he said. "They were just going to recharge when we ran into that mine. Blaine says we have only enough juice to last us two hours, moderate running."

He paused for a moment as Ted grasped the significance of the situation.

"Furthermore," Sammy continued, "we cannot dive to any considerable depth."

"With that leak in the reservoir plates Cleary and Blame say it would be foolhardy to go down very far for fear the Dewey would spread wide open and we would be flooded."

It was disquieting news, and Ted hurried forward to talk it over with Jack. As he passed the control station he saw Cleary and Binns in animated conference with the chief engineer. He surmised they were debating the best course under the circumstances.

In the bunk room Ted found Jack had revived considerably under the influence of hot bouillon and strong coffee provided by Jean Cartier, and a change of clothing with a stiff rub-down that had done wonders for him.

"Monsieur is a brave man; he wins the American Croix de Guerre for saving the life of his commander so bravely," Jean was saying as Ted reappeared upon the scene.

Jack was trying hard to be modest.

"I'm feeling fine again, chum," was his rejoinder in response to Ted's query. "Come along. I'm going to look in on 'Little Mack.'" And grabbing Ted's arm he walked off with him to the lieutenant's quarters.

They found McClure now conscious, but very faint from his ordeal. It was certain that he could not assume command of the Dewey for some time.

The boys clambered on deck to unlimber a bit. Executive Officer Cleary was in charge. In the commotion attendant upon the collision with the mine and the rescue of the submarine commander the disabled German cruiser had been forgotten. There was now no trace of the doomed ship nor of the English "limey" that had been standing by.

"What do you suppose we will do now?" asked Ted.

"Reckon we'll have to drift around awhile and wait for somebody to come along and give us a lift," said Jack hopefully.

Night came on, but there was no response to the wireless call of the Dewey. Once a "limey" was spoken, but signaled in return that she was speeding to the assistance of a Scandinavian liner that had reported being under the shell fire of a German U-boat.

Jack was ordered to turn in right after evening "chow" despite his insistence that he was perfectly recovered from his dip in the sea. Ted was to report to the conning tower at four bells for duty on watch.

All night long the Dewey tossed in a rough sea. At the appointed hour Ted took up his station as lookout in the conning tower. He had instructions to maintain a sharp watch for enemy ships and to keep Acting Commander Cleary informed on all wireless registrations. The hours passed slowly.

Presently a storm rolled up out of the North Sea. Forked lightning and the distant rumble of thunder heralded its advance. The breeze increased to a gale before long and the sea became rough and angry.

Awakened by the tossing of the little craft and the ominous thunder, Jack appeared in the conning tower. Saluting the ship's executive officer, he declared he was feeling quite recovered from his strenuous dip in the sea of the previous day and quite ready for any service. Jack, accordingly, was posted at the reserve periscope. Ted was at the observation ports in the tower and Officer Cleary at the other periscope.

As the storm increased in fury the Dewey was buffeted about like an egg shell.

Ted was nursing a severe bump on the head, having been dashed by the rocking of the boat against one of the steel girders. Hanging on to supports, the crew of the Dewey were having a hard time saving life and limb as they were tossed to and fro by the fury of the storm.

When at last dawn broke over the troubled waters the gale began to subside. Even then it was impossible to lift the hatches and go on deck because of the rough sea. Waves mountain high were rolling over the submarine, and to open the conning tower was to invite certain disaster. There was nothing to do but wait.

Toward six o'clock Ted made out a long rakish-looking craft that had come up out of the southwest. When it was reported to Officer Cleary and he had looked critically at the vessel for some time he declared finally that it was a destroyer, but yet too far off to hazard any guess as to its nationality.

He decided to submerge slightly and watch the craft for a while and, if it proved to be a German warship, to submerge entirely and take chances on the leaky fuel reservoirs. The Dewey sank at his direction until the conning tower was under water.

"It looks like a French vessel," declared the acting commander to Jack a few minutes later as the warship came nearer.

He studied the approaching ship for a few minutes. "We will raise the lid of the conning tower and unfurl the Stars and Stripes from the periscope pole," he said finally.

"If it is a French destroyer we will soon find out; if it proves to be a German vessel let's hope we will have time to submerge and give him a torpedo. Will you take the flag aloft, Mr. Wainwright?" asked the Dewey's officer.

Saluting, Ted took the proffered flag and declared he was ready to start forthwith.

Making a slip knot of the line, he motioned for the hatch to be lifted and raised himself out of the turret as the lid swung upward.

The waves were dashing against the projection of steel and lashed their salty spray over the lad as he wrapped his legs about the slippery pole and began to climb. It was difficult work as the vessel lurched in the turbulent sea, but Ted persevered and succeeded in throwing the noose over the end of the pole above the eye of the periscope. Sliding deftly back again, unfurling the flag as he came, he was soon safe again in the conning tower.

Maneuvering about for a few minutes in a frantic effort to attract the attention of the unknown ship, the Dewey was finally rewarded by the boom of a gun that was followed almost immediately by the breaking out of the tricolor of France.

"Vive la France!" shouted the excited group in the conning tower of the Dewey. The cry spread throughout the hold and there was great rejoicing among the badly battered seasick prisoners within the stranded submarine.

Still on guard against trickery, the destroyer approached warily with all guns trained on the Dewey. Jean Cartier was called into the conning tower and as the destroyer drew within range poured a volley of joyous French expletives into the megaphone that had been thrust into his hand. In short order the submarine had completely established her identity and acquainted the commander of the destroyer with the condition of affairs aboard the Dewey.

The French vessel proved to be the La Roque, and her commander gladly consented to tow the disabled American vessel into an English port. Commander McClure was made as comfortable as possible and the voyage across the North Sea begun.

The disabled submarine weathered the trip very well and was delivered safely at an English base by the La Roque after an uneventful voyage.

Granted a shore furlough, Jack and Ted jumped a train and went up to London for their first visit in the famous city. For several days they took in the sights of the great metropolis, seeing, among other things, a wonderful reception accorded American troops from the States marching in review before King George on their way to the front, visiting Westminster Abbey and other notable places, looking in on the House of Commons for several hours and visiting the American embassy.

Letters awaited them from Brighton and they read with interest of the enlistment of more of their chums in the various branches of their country's service. Not the least important of their surprises was a great box from home filled with warm clothing, cakes, candies, and "eats" aplenty.

When they reported back again at their ship they found that the Dewey, slightly damaged, had been put into drydock and repairs were going steadily ahead. To their great joy they learned that Lieutenant McClure had not been injured seriously and was convalescing in a nearby hospital. They visited "Little Mack," who by now had heard the whole story of his rescue. Tears dimmed the eyes of the little commander as he expressed his thanks to Jack and Ted for their plucky part in hauling him back to safety after the fateful mine explosion.

By the time the repairs to the Dewey had been completed Lieutenant

McClure was able to assume command of his gallant little ship.

Soon came orders for the Dewey to proceed to sea again. This time the submarine was to act jointly with a convoy protecting the passage of troopships across the English Channel to Calais, and thence into action off Zeebrugge against the German destroyers making that port their rendezvous.

CHAPTER X

ATTACKED FROM THE SKY

On a wonderful September evening, with a crisp autumnal air making every fellow feel like a young kitten, the Dewey again glided away from her anchorage in the harbor of Chatham, one of the important English naval bases, and fell into her position in the convoy of ships spread out as an escort for a trio of troopships. They were crowded with thousands of young chaps, the majority of them Americans and Canadians, on their way to join the armies "somewhere in France."

Bronzed and sturdy as a result of their summer's training in home waters and their activities aboard the submarine in the North Sea, Jack and Ted stood out on the deck of their craft more eager than ever to get back into active service again, notwithstanding the rigors of the service in which they had enlisted.

"Little Mack," now completely recovered from his injuries, was in command again and smiling good naturedly at "his boys" as they stood grouped about on the deck of the Dewey.

They were thrilled with the anticipation of marvelous new exploits in which they were likely to participate, now that the United States had sent a naval commission to cooperate with the London admiralty and the French naval experts in what was expected to be a campaign to carry the war by naval tactics right home to Germany.

"Ain't no use in expecting that German navy to come out in the open and fight to a finish," commented Bill Witt, as the conversation turned on the likelihood of a big battle between the German high seas fleet and the combined fleets of the United States, Great Britain, and France. "Those fellows would sooner lay back safe in the Kiel Canal; they know full well we'd make short work of them if they ever came outside."

"Ten to one your Uncle Sam don't wait for them to come outside," put in Jack earnestly. "Now that they have all got together and figured out what to do as a result of the sessions of that joint naval board in London, we're likely to be sent right in after them."

Jack's eyes glowed as he thought of the daring feats possible under such a naval policy.

"You can bet the Dewey will be in on any such stunts as that," pursued Ted. "And why shouldn't we go right after them? The United States Navy never did lie back and wait for the enemy to come out."

Passing along, the deck to the conning tower, Lieutenant McClure stopped to eye the little group.

"You fellows just aching for a scrap again," he said finally. "Well, there's no telling when we might run right into one to-night. Those German destroyers are likely to make a sortie from Ostend. Besides, you never can tell when some of the Kaiser's air navy is likely to be popping around."

As he spoke "Little Mack" scanned the sky to the east. Turning to the boys, he remarked laughingly: "You three pretty good chums, aren't you?" gazing along the line, from Jack to Ted and then to Bill Witt.

"Just like three peas in a pod," declared Bill Witt. "These two Brighton boys took me right in—-and me a rank outsider! I'm sure lucky to have struck two such good friends."

Everybody laughed at Bill's frank avowal of friendship and Jack responded with a crack on the back that made Bill wince.

"Guess we know good goods when we meet it," he added.

"Little Mack" had been taking it all in with approval.

"That's right, boys," he smiled. "You've got the right spirit. That's the kind of democracy we stand for, and that's why the good old U.S. Navy is the best in the world—-fellows all pulling together. I'm mighty proud of all my boys," continued the little lieutenant. "You've made a great record so far, and I only hope you keep up the good work. Stick together like pals—-and be proud of that flag of ours."

With a wave of the hand the ship's commander passed along the deck and into the conning tower.

"There's an ace for you," said Jack, with an admiring glance at the retreating figure.

"Ace! I should say so," sputtered Bill. "Why, if 'Little Mack' told me to go get von Tirpitz I'd go right after him."

Soon it was dusk and the little fleet had gotten out of sight of land into the North Sea. Stealing away like shadows into the gloom, the fleet of transports trailed along in battle formation ready to turn back any attack. The crew of the Dewey had retreated into the hold and the vessel was riding awash, with Commander McClure at the wheel, observing the deployment of the fleet from the conning tower.

Down in the torpedo room, bottled up under water where no sound could escape to attract the attention of the outside world, Mike Mowrey had tuned up his old banjo and the boys were having an old-fashioned songfest.

"For it's always fair weather," came the jolly strains that sounded up in the conning tower above the whirr of the ship's engines.

"Everybody's happy to get out again," laughed Executive Officer Cleary to his chief, as he swung the periscope to port for a full sweep of the sea.

So far there had been no incident to mar the safe convoy of the troopships. Plowing straight ahead, the destroyers that flitted here and there through the filmy darkness danced about the transports, alert to challenge any foe. Another hour and the short trip to the French port where the troops were to embark would be concluded and the Dewey free to dash off to her post along the Belgian coast, where Commander McClure had been ordered on guard against the German destroyers that lately had been showing a desire to engage in brushes with the allied ships.

"Guess we are not going to be molested to-night," said "Little Mack" as he looked at his wrist watch.

"Doesn't seem like it," rejoined Cleary.

But they had reckoned without the two-mile-a-minute birdmen that circle the heavens like giant eagles and swoop down on their prey from high altitudes to send forth their flaming bombs and death-dealing hand grenades. A lookout on one of the destroyers detected at this moment an aerial fleet looming out of the north like spectral dots in the dim light of the skies. From the masthead of the vessel glowed instantly the light that had been agreed upon as a danger signal.

"Airplanes!" shouted the Dewey's commander, as he strained his eyes through the portholes of the conning tower in a vain effort to search the skies. In another moment, after giving the "wheel" over to his flag officer, the lieutenant had thrown open the conning tower and was gazing into the heavens with his binoculars.

"Yes, there they come," he announced, after a short pause. "Two—-three—-four; there's a half dozen or more of them," he continued after a careful survey of the sky.

The singing down in the hold abated when the reported approach of the air fleet became known throughout the ship.

"What's up?" queried Ted, as he joined his chum outside the wireless room.

"The Kaiser's imperial flying corps is out for a little evening exercise," answered Jack, as he hurried along to keep within call of his commander.

For the men in the Dewey there was nothing to do but take the reports from the conning tower as to what was going on outside the submarine. Their impatience, however, was short-lived, for there came very quickly an order to man the anti-aircraft guns on deck. The hatches fore and aft were thrown open and the gun crews scrambled on deck.

"Not afraid of 'em, are we?" chuckled Ted, as he followed Bill Witt up the ladder.

"Chances are they can't see us in the twilight," answered Bill. "And this is a real chance for us to give the 'twins' a little tuning up."

From the conning tower came the order to unlimber the guns, load and stand by.

"Wait until they come within range, and then fire away!" directed the Dewey's commander.

From a height of five thousand feet the leader of the "air cavalry" suddenly turned the nose of his craft downward, and came volplaning toward the sea at a dizzy pace. Following suit, the remaining units of the attacking squadron dived to get within better range.

"Now, boys!" shouted Lieutenant McClure.

Time-fuse shells had been inserted in the "Twins," the breeches closed and the muzzles elevated to point at the fast-flying airships. At the aft gun Ted gripped the trigger ready to fire, while Mike Mowrey jammed his good right eye into the telescopic sight to make sure of his aim.

"Fire!" he yelled, and Ted, let her go. The shot sped away into the sky while the crew gazed eagerly upward to watch for the explosion. Soon the shell burst with a white puff of smoke.

"Little too far to the right," said the observer.

Now the aft gun spoke. From every vessel of the protecting fleet came answering shots as they belched their fury at the armada of the air. The dull gray of the night sky was lighted at intervals by the bursting of shells as the German air fleet soared forward over the allied naval fleet. Observers were hurling bombs from above and they were splashing into the sea on every side. One of them striking the hull of the Dewey would blow the ship into atoms!

"Keep it up, boys! Make every shot count!" sang out Commander McClure.

Mike Mowrey was growling because he was unable to make a hit. "Let's get one of 'em—-just one of 'em!" he bellowed in rage.

One of the winged fleet was circling almost overhead at this moment and seemed tantalizing near. With a twist of the wheel Mowrey swung the muzzle of his gun up a couple of inches and gave the signal again to fire. Following the shot for a moment the frenzied gunner was elated to note that the machine just above sagged suddenly to one side. Like a bird with a broken pinion it swerved drunkenly in its course and began slowly to come down. Sustaining wires had been cut by the shell fire from the Dewey and the airplane was out of commission.

"Guess that fellow is done for," said Mowrey.

It was soon evident that the machine was badly crippled, for it came on downward like a feather floating in the still air. Only a few minutes elapsed until it had settled on the water.

"Hydro-aeroplane," announced Commander McClure as he stood in the conning tower observing the wounded airship. The other planes were engaged over the remainder of the allied fleet and the Dewey was free to take care of the craft in front of it.

There was now a chance that the American submarine might move alongside and take prisoner the German birdmen in the damaged machine. The ship's course was altered toward the floating plane and the Dewey crept up on her foe.

"Train your forward gun right on that fellow; he is apt to shoot unless both pilot and observer are injured," cautioned McClure.

And that was just what happened, for the words had hardly escaped the lips of the Yankee skipper before a gun rang out from under the canvas wings of the airplane and a shell came whizzing over the Dewey.

"There's another machine almost directly overhead," bawled Mowrey, as he spied a second flying craft near at hand.

Having witnessed the fall of the crippled airship, another member of the attacking squadron had put back to the rescue. As it soared now within range of the American submarine a bomb came splashing into the water not two hundred feet away.

Commander McClure began to figure that it was getting too dangerous longer to risk his thin-skinned vessel before the rain of the lyddite bombs, and accordingly gave orders to submerge. Jamming their guns back into their deck casings, the crews melted away through the hatches into the hold of the Dewey. Ballast poured in through the valves and the ship began to submerge.

And then, just as the submarine began settling in the water, a shell came whizzing over the water from the wounded airplane and burst directly over the conning tower. There was a crash of rending steel and then a great clatter on the forward deck of the submarine that reechoed through the interior with an ominous sound.

"Great Scott!" ejaculated McClure. "They've torn away both our periscopes!"

CHAPTER XI

IN THE FOG

Completely blinded by the fire from the wounded German birdman, the Dewey now had but one alternative. The approach of other air raiders made it necessary for the submarine to dive away into the depths to safety. To linger longer on the surface was but to court the continued fire of the birdmen overhead who apparently were incensed over the wounding of their companion craft and out for revenge.

Reluctantly, but yielding to his better judgment, McClure gave orders to submerge. At the same time the damaged periscopes were cut off in the conning tower to prevent an inflow of water when the ship dived.

"Too bad to quit right now; but it would be folly to stand out under those deadly bombs any longer," he said.

Fortunately, the Dewey was equipped with reserve periscope tubes, and Lieutenant McClure's plan now was to wait until the convenient darkness of night had mantled the ocean and then ascend to repair at leisure the damaged "eyes."

"Might as well make ourselves comfortable here awhile under the water," suggested "Little Mack."

Jean Cartier was instructed to extend himself for the evening meal and to draw on the ship's larder for an "extra fine dinner." It being the first night of the Dewey's renewed cruise the ship's galley was well stocked with fresh foods. Chops, baked potatoes, hot tea and rice pudding represented the menu selected by Jean, and soon the odor of the savory food had every mother's son smacking his lips in anticipation of a luxurious "chow" to top off the exciting events of the evening.

Seventy feet below the surface of the water, immune from hostile attacks, officers and crew sat down to the repast as safe and secure as though in a banquet hail on shore. Wit and laughter accompanied the courses, and, as the submarine dinner was concluded, Bill Witt's banjo was produced. Soon the ship resounded to the "plink-plunk-plink" of the instrument and the gay songs of the jolly submarine sailors.

"If they could only see us now at Brighton!" laughed Ted, as he surveyed the scene admiringly.

Jack grew reminiscent.

"Remember that last dinner at Brighton?" he asked. "Fellows all wishing us good luck and cheering for us out on the campus? And good old 'prexie' declaring he expected to hear great things of his boys in the war? And all of them standing on the dormitory steps singing 'Fair Brighton' as we headed for the depot?"

Ted remembered it all now only too plainly. Good old Brighton! Back there now under the oaks on the campus, or up in the dormitories, the boys were assembled again for the fall term.

But this was not the time for backward glances. Grim work lay ahead of them.

An hour later preparations were made to ascend and repair the damaged periscopes. In response to a query from the ship's commander, Sammy Smith said he could find no trace of any nearby or approaching vessels, although he had given the submarine telephone its best test.

Gradually the Dewey came to the surface as the ballast tanks were emptied. The hatch was thrown open and the Dewey's commander raised himself to get a line on his surroundings.

A dense fog had commenced to settle over the water, blotting out the stars and making a mist that hung over the sea like a great gray blanket.

"Could not be better for our purposes had it been made to order," smiled McClure, as he gave orders for the repair crew to haul out the reserve periscopes and get busy.

It was impossible to see more than a hundred yards from the sides of the Dewey in any direction, and there appeared nothing but the rolling swell of the ocean. Nevertheless, overlooking no precaution, McClure gave orders for all lights to be dimmed amidships. In the darkness the crew went to work to substitute the new "eyes" of the ship for the damaged tubes, climbing out on the superstructure and working energetically.

Just as the forward periscope was being lowered into position and secured, Commander McClure, supervising the work, was startled by a voice out of the fog, a stentorian challenge through a megaphone, that seemed almost on top of the submarine.

"What ship is that?" came the call in German.

For a moment it seemed that some one on the deck of the submarine must be playing a prank on his friends. But Bill Witt, who was doing lookout duty forward, declared that the cry was right at hand and apparently from the deck of a warship.

Whispering to the repair crew to go quickly below McClure addressed himself to the unknown voice in his best Deutsch.

"Dis iss das unterseeboot nein und zwanzig."

For a moment there was a deathless silence. Then again the heavy voice to port:

"You speck not the truth. U-boat 29 is in der Kiel Canal. You are

English or Yankee. We call on you to surrender!"

McClure's answer was to slam down the lid of the conning tower and ring for full speed in the engine room. Instantly he switched the rudder to starboard as the Dewey's propeller blades began to turn.

"Dive!" yelled the commander to his navigating officer, as he himself slanted the submerging rudders.

Almost at the same moment the German warship's powerful searchlights turned full upon the American submarine. Then came a great spit of fire from a battery aboard the enemy vessel followed by the roar of her guns and a salvo of shots.

"It's no use, boys," said the submarine commander to his officers. "They have us trapped. Unless we surrender here we are going to be blown out of the water in short order. We cannot submerge quick enough to avoid that terrible gunfire."

Again and a shot from the enemy, and this time it struck in the water just in front of the conning tower and flung a great spray that blinded the portholes.

The Dewey was just starting to submerge. With her diving rudders inclined, the ship was tilted now until her bow pointed downward and her stern reared up out of the water. She was shipping ballast in her tanks rapidly, but the process was necessarily slow and, even with her improved equipment, it must be one and a half to two minutes before the hull could be submerged, let alone the conning tower.

"Hold her right there!" suddenly shouted the young lieutenant to his navigating officer.

The latter was for a moment completely dumbfounded by the order.

"What—-you don't mean—-why—-" he started to say, but instantly withheld his speech at the frowning face of his superior officer.

"Up with that hatch!" the Dewey's commander thundered, as his executive officer stood aghast at the reckless procedure.

The latter hastened, however, to comply with the order.

"Wainwright!" shouted Lieutenant McClure.

Ted jumped into the conning tower beside his commander.

"You have already shown your bravery," began McClure hurriedly. "Here's another test for you. Climb through the conning tower, run forward and dive off the bow. But, first of all, grab a life-belt and strap it to you. Don't ask questions. Have confidence in me. When you get in the water, work your way rapidly around the bow of the Dewey to starboard. Float there in the shadow of our hull. Keep close up. All will be well in a moment."

Obeying orders implicitly, Ted was strapping on the life-preserver.

"Ready?" called McClure.

Ted saluted.

"Right—-go!" shouted the commander of the Dewey.

CHAPTER XII

YANKEE CAMOUFLAGE

To Ted it seemed as though he were following the mandate of some madman as he emerged from the conning tower and, grasping the periscope pole, steadied himself a moment before leaping down on deck. But, being a loyal son of Uncle Sam, and realizing that the first requisite of a sailor was to take orders implicitly from his officers, he sprang nimbly on deck, rushed along the inclined steel plane, and as he came splashing into the water that washed over the bow, flung himself into the sea.

"I'll trust to 'Little Mack'," he said to himself.

Coming up to the surface he veered off sharp to the Dewey's starboard and with long strokes pulled himself into the shadow of the partially submerged submarine. The life-belt held him secure in the water and he floated at ease.

Ted turned his attention toward the Dewey.

There, he saw, his example was being followed by other members of the crew. As their names were called off by their commander a number of the crew leaped overboard.

One stood up on the rim of the conning tower and dived away from the glare of the enemy searchlights into the black shadows of the submarine. Suddenly the aft hatch was thrown open directly above the engine room and in a moment several begrimed members of the engine crew scrambled up the ladder in quick succession and threw themselves into the sea. The enemy had ceased firing.

"What does it all mean?" pondered Ted as he floated, watching the graphic picture.

Unable to solve the problem for himself, he turned his attention to the nearest man in the water. He swam now only a few strokes away. With little effort Ted drew up to him. It was Bill Witt.

"Reckon they rammed a shot into her," yelled Bill as they beheld their ship sinking gradually.

"Looks that way, doesn't it?" answered Ted

The stricken submarine was gradually going down. McClure was there in the conning tower, of course; that old tradition of the sea, about every skipper going down with his ship, held true in the case of a submarine as well. Jack was there, too, in all likelihood; he had been standing by his commander as Ted and Bill hurried up to hurl themselves from the deck. Ted gulped as he thought of his chum. Was it all over with Jack? Would the Germans rescue the American lads bobbing about in the water?

In another moment the Dewey was completely under, leaving many of her crew floating in the open sea, at the mercy of their enemies.

"Tough luck!" stammered Ted as he linked arms with Bill over their life-belts.

Bill was dauntless even in the face of death.

"You never can tell," he said. "I am guessing that 'Little Mack' has another card up his sleeve."

Down in the turret of the submerged Dewey an extraordinary scene was being enacted. McClure, Cleary and Jack were standing together as the vessel glided away under the water.

"It worked—-it worked!" shouted the young lieutenant as he ordered the submerging process discontinued and the Dewey held on an even keel.

"What worked?" gasped his dazed executive, who had yet to grasp the significance of his commander's action in ordering members of the crew overboard.

"Why, don't you see? Those Germans think they sank us. When they saw our boys leaping into the water they took it for granted one of their shots had landed and we were done for. They think the boys leaped overboard to escape death in the hold of a mortally wounded Yankee. And here we are, safe and sound, under the water!"

"But what about those fellows swimming around up there?" asked Jack in startled tones.

"We'll go back and get them in a few minutes after we've tended to this Prussian gentleman that we hypnotized," shot back his commander, as his jaw squared and his eyes flashed.

Jack and Officer Cleary stared at each other.

"Well, of all the nerve!" gasped Cleary.

"Great Scott, man! it takes a real honest-to-goodness Yankee like you to get away with such a trick."

Veering off to port, the skipper steered a straight course for several hundred yards. Then the Dewey cut out into a short half circle and in another moment came to a stop sixty-five feet below the surface.

"Put her up," came the order to the navigating officer at the ship's air pumps.

There was an interval of strained silence as the commander waited until the eye of the periscope had cleared the spray that dashed against the glass.

"There they are!" he announced. "Light still turned on the spot where we went down a minute or so ago. Guess they are waiting to see whether we really are done for."

A signal to the Dewey's engine rooms put the vessel in motion just long enough for her commander to turn the nose of the craft slightly to starboard, and then the submarine rested quietly again.

"Friends, Americans, and fellow patriots: my compliments to the Imperial German Navy," began "Little Mack" as he leaned forward to touch off a torpedo—-and there was a rare smile on his lips.

For an instant the Dewey quivered as the torpedo shot from the bow of the submerged ship and raced away under the water. Her commander hugged the periscope glass and watched for developments.

"Got him!" he shouted excitedly, dancing about wildly on the grating of the conning tower. "It's a hit beyond all doubt. We struck her almost amidships."

The German vessel had been dealt a deathblow. She was sending up distress signals.

"She's afire now and can't last long," mused the Dewey's commander as he continued to survey the ship in distress. "Her magazines will go in a minute."

The chief concern of the Dewey now was the reclaiming of her sailors from the sea.

There was little likelihood of gun fire from the sinking German warship. Her crew were bent on launching lifeboats and getting away before the final plunge that would carry the ship down to the bottom. Accordingly, the Yankee submarine came to the surface and commenced preparations for the rescue of her own crew. Lights were hung at the mastheads fore and aft and a huge searchlight hurriedly adjusted on the forepart of the conning tower and the electrical connections made amidships.

Out of the mist that overhung the sea burst forth suddenly a great glare. Through the fog loomed a white mass of flame like the blast of a thousand furnaces, with tongues of fire piercing the night gloom. The sea was rocked by an explosion that reverberated over the waters like the crash of a million guns and tossed the submarine like a piece of driftwood.

"One less warship for the Kaiser's navy," remarked McClure.

"And all because of your rare cunning, old boy," countered his executive enthusiastically.

Out of the darkness came a shout for help close at hand. Switching the searchlight in the direction of the cry, Commander McClure beheld a head bobbing in the water only a few yards away. It was one of his own crew, one of the electrician's helpers who had gone overboard with the rest in the mad scramble to outwit the Germans. In a few minutes he was hauled aboard, dripping wet, his teeth chattering from the exposure in the water.

"They are all around here," the boy chattered. "We managed to keep pretty close together in the water."

McClure grasped his hand.

"You are a brave lad," he said. "Every man of you has proved his mettle by taking a daring chance. Go below now, son, get into warm clothing and gets something hot to drink."

Coasting to and fro in the water, scanning the sea now to the right, now to the left, the Dewey continued the search for her crew.

Singly, in twos, and in one case three, men were picked up until it seemed to the commander that every boy who had gone overboard had been reclaimed from the sea.

"Call the roll below decks," the commander instructed his executive officer. Jack and his commander remained in the conning tower still operating the searchlight.

In a few minutes Officer Cleary returned.

"All safe?" asked "Little Mack."

"No; two still missing," was the executive officer's reply.

"Who are they?" McClure queried.

"Ted Wainwright and Bill Witt," came the answer.

CHAPTER XIII

THE SURVIVORS

Jack's knees sagged for a moment and it seemed his heart stood still.

His old Brighton chum and good old Bill Witt still unaccounted for!

Out there in the dark and the water somewhere they were floating alone!

Then he heard "Little Mack" speaking.

"We'll stay right here until we find them," he was saying.

Megaphones were brought on deck and the Dewey's officers began calling into the darkness of the sea. Another searchlight was run up through the stern hatch and affixed aft to sweep the sea from that end of the vessel. For a time there was no response to their calls; then, when it seemed that all hope had fled, there came a hoarse cry, now seeming far away, now closer and louder.

"Something there to starboard just off our bow!" shouted Jack, who had climbed up on the conning tower.

McClure directed that both searchlights be flashed in the direction of the muffled calls and was rewarded by the faint outlines of a small boat buffeted about in the water like a cork.

"Well, they are not our boys," said the Dewey's skipper listlessly.

Then, taking Jack's megaphone, he shouted: "Who are you?"

A tail, gaunt figure loomed up in the bow of the lifeboat. He was waving a life-belt frantically with an appealing gesture for aid.

"Survivors from der German gunboat Strassburg," came the reply in broken English.

McClure ordered them to come alongside and cautioned his men to be on guard against any surprise attack.

Out of the gloom came the lifeboat like a weird specter, propelled by the sweeping oars of half a dozen frantically working seamen. It was crowded with a motley crew of bedraggled sailors. They presented a pitiable spectacle as their craft slowly made its way toward the Dewey and into the bright rays from the searchlights.

"We have two of your men in here," shouted the leader of the party, who was evidently an officer of the sunken warship. At the same time two boys well to the stern waved their arms frantically toward the group on the conning tower of the Dewey.

"Here I am, Jack, and Bill Witt is right with me," came the familiar voice of Ted Wainwright.

"Hurrah!" the cry arose from the deck of the American submersible. Overcome with joy, Jack could scarce restrain his emotions as he clutched the periscope pole and shielded his eyes with his other hand to make sure that his ears had not deceived him. Yes, it was Ted—-and there was Bill just behind him!

Making its way clumsily forward, the boat finally drew up alongside.

Willing hands helped Ted and Bill up the steep side of the Dewey

and they were tendered such a reception as they had never known before.

Then ensued a parley between the petty officer of the sunken gunboat

Strassburg and the commander of the Dewey.

"We are very happy to be your prisoners, under the circumstances," began the German officer in his best English.

"I thank you for rescuing my men," said McClure. "Sorry I can't take you aboard, but I'll tow you to the Dutch coast or transfer you to the first inbound trader. Satisfactory?"

"Thank you, sir," said the German.

Before making fast the towline from the lifeboat to the stern of the Dewey for the journey toward the coast McClure had Jean Cartier and his commissary assistant bring up pots of steaming hot coffee and dole it out to the forlorn Teutons.

Jack went below with Ted and Bill Witt to hear the story of their escape. It appeared that they had floated around together in the dark; had witnessed the sinking of the gunboat Strassburg and, when it went down, had been caught in the swell of the water and carried far from the lights of the Dewey. They had seen the submarine when it turned on its powerful searchlights.

"Bill and I thought we were done for," said Ted between gulps of coffee. "We had just about given up for good. We tried to swim, but our clothes and the life-belts weighed us down, and our legs and arms were so cramped we couldn't make any headway. Then while we were trying to keep our eyes on the faint lights of the Dewey, what should we see but a boat steering right at us! Without any words, the Germans stooped right down and dragged us into their boat. None of us could see each other very well, but we soon made out they were Germans. They discovered our nationality about the same time and they wouldn't believe us when we told them we were from the U.S. submarine that had sunk them."

"Did they try anything rough on you?" put in Jack.

"No," continued Ted, "they were so thankful to be in that boat instead of floundering in the sea they didn't care much about anything else. When we told them our vessel was somewhere close by they wouldn't believe it until we showed them the faint streaks of light from the Dewey through the fog. Then Bill Witt told them they would stand a better chance for their lives if they got in touch with the American submarine. They parleyed a while over that and finally decided they would take Bill's tip. That's how we got up within range of you fellows and got back here again. We might have floated around all night and been picked up in the morning and then again we might not."

"Well, I'm glad you're back again, chum," added Jack with an affectionate hug. He now hurried back to the conning tower to be within call of his commanders. The Dewey was headed due east; running on the surface, with her boatload of prisoners trailing behind.

Two hours' running brought the Dewey within the ten-mile zone of the Dutch coast, and suddenly she ran into the hail of a huge brigantine that appeared to be becalmed. She lay quiet in the water without a tangible sign of life except her binnacle lights.

Watchful against any deception, McClure ordered the gun crews on deck and the "Twins" ready for action. Then he challenged the sailing craft.

The answer came in German. Likely the watch thought his vessel had been approached by a U-boat of the Central Powers. Challenged again in English, the fellow went below and returned in a moment with an English-speaking companion. Lieutenant McClure briefly made known his desire to turn over the German prisoners.

"But we don't want them," came the reply.

Jack and Ted, standing out on deck together, grinned. This seemed so unlike Dutch hospitality.

"Holland doesn't seem to be so fond of Germans, does she?" joked Jack.

"Can't much blame them," Ted replied soberly. "They have enough mouths of their own to feed without any more outsiders."

Lieutenant McClure insisted, however, on putting the Germans aboard the brigantine and finally won out. The lifeboat went alongside and the Dewey stood by until every Teuton had climbed up the side.

"Auf Wiedersehen and thank you, sir," called the German officer as the Dewey backed away and turned her nose out to sea again.

The days that followed were crowded with colorful incidents for the band of Americans aboard the gallant little submarine. With the arrival of Uncle Sam's submarines in the North Sea and their active participation in the warfare against the Imperial German Navy the forages of the cruiser and destroyer raiders out of Wilhelmshaven and other German ports were decreasing in number.

The Belgian coast is but forty-two miles long, extending from Zeebrugge at the northern extremity to Ostend—-the Atlantic City of Belgium—-at the south, but there are a number of tiny harbors along the strip of coastline, and these were infested by the light draft German warships, particularly the destroyers. The American submarines in particular were directing their attention toward these destroyers and seeking to kill them off as they dashed out of their "fox holes" for flying attacks against the allied navies.

One night, after a quiet day on patrol off the Belgian coast, the Dewey settled for the night close to shore at a point about five miles southwest of the Belgian coast town of Blankenberghe, a tiny fishing port with a small and almost land-locked harbor. It was a strategic position directly on the course that would be taken by German destroyers out of Zeebrugge bound for a raid off Dunkirk or Calais. Lying under the sea, the Dewey could hear approaching vessels.

Furthermore, Lieutenant McClure had reason to believe that German destroyers were making a rendezvous of the little harbor of Blankenberghe. He was determined to find out and to "get somebody."

Jack was on duty in the conning tower and Executive Officer Cleary in the control chamber underneath. Floating here at a depth of one hundred and ten feet the Dewey was to spend the night resting and with a vigilant ear for any passing vessels.

Thousands of miles from home, more then a hundred feet deep down in the North Sea, bottled up in a submarine while the rest of his churns slept peacefully as though at home in their beds, the Brighton boy sat alone in the conning tower of the submerged Dewey.

"Some difference between where I am now and where I was a year ago this time!" he was reflecting, when he heard the night wireless operator reporting to Executive Officer Cleary the approach of a vessel overhead.

Jack descended into the control chamber and, at Officer Cleary's direction, called Lieutenant McClure, who had turned in for several hours' rest, leaving instructions that he be aroused in case any ships were reported overhead.

CHAPTER XIV

ON THE BOTTOM OF THE SEA

Listening for a few moments at the microphones, McClure turned abruptly and rang the crew to quarters.

The engine room was signaled to tune up the motors.

"From the way that fellow is hugging the coast I wouldn't be surprised if he is a Hun raider poking along on a little reconnaissance," observed McClure to his executive officer.

Aroused from his slumber, Sammy Smith took charge of the electrical receiving room and after listening for awhile gave his opinion that the approaching ship was moving south along the Belgian coast and distant from the Dewey about a mile and a half. From the faint registrations in the microphones he judged it to be a vessel of light draft—-probably a small cruiser or a destroyer.

"Well, we never lose an opportunity to do our duty, be the enemy large or small fry," observed McClure.

After waiting for a few moments longer, and being advised of the continued steady approach of the ship, the young lieutenant decided to move in closer to get within better range, and then rise to the surface and "look her over." It was well on toward four o'clock and soon would be daylight.

Creeping along at half speed, the Dewey veered slightly to starboard and steered a course N.N.W. toward the oncoming craft. After cruising thus for a quarter of an hour the submarine was stopped altogether again and her captain conferred again with his wireless chief.

"She seems to have changed her course," announced Smith after listening intently at both port and starboard microphones. "As near as I can calculate she has turned off abruptly to port and is running due east toward the coast."

"Fine!" exclaimed McClure. "A German for sure. And now perhaps we can track her to her lair."

In a few moments the Dewey thrust her periscopes up out of the sea and set out in pursuit of the unknown ship. It was yet too dark to make her out, except for a dim blur that showed faintly against the background of the Belgian coast. By striking the Dewey's latitude and longitude they figured they were at a point five or six miles off Blankenberghe.

"Where do you suppose she is heading for?" asked Cleary. He was plainly puzzled.

"There probably is a canal near at hand that the Germans have dug out since their occupation of Belgium, and which they now are using as a retreat for their light draft vessels—-possibly a submarine base," answered McClure.

For a time the Dewey followed steadily on in the wake of the German. It was not long until McClure, at the forward periscope, was able to get a better look at the foe.

"A big destroyer," he announced. "I can make out her four funnels."

It was now apparent to the lieutenant that they were approaching close to the coast and that very shortly the destroyer must turn again to the sea or else take her way into some tortuous channel leading inland.

"Reckon we have gone as far as we can," he declared after a further observation. He had in mind the fact that the approach to the waterway for which the destroyer was headed most certainly was mined and that without a chart of the course he was running the risk of driving into one of the dangerous buoys.

He determined to chance a shot at the destroyer, submerge and go out to sea again. Sighting on the dimly outlined destroyer he released a torpedo and then, without waiting to observe the result of the random shot, gave the signal to dive.

Down went the Dewey. And in another moment, as the gallant sub slipped away into the depths, she lurched suddenly with a staggering motion and brought up sharp with an impact that shook the vessel from stem to stern. Officer Cleary was catapulted off his feet and crashed into the steel conning tower wall, with an exclamation of pain. The Dewey seemed to have run hard against an undersea wall.

"Reverse the engine!" shouted McClure. "We must have run upon a sandy shoal."

Frantically he rang the engine room to back away. But the order came too late. With a slow ringing noise that plainly bespoke the grating of the ship's keel on the bed of the ocean the submarine slid forward and then came to a dead stop, quivering in every steel plate from the tremendous throbbing of her engines.

"Great Scott, we've run aground!" exclaimed McClure as he stood wild-eyed in the conning tower.

Jack was despatched to the engine room for a report from Chief Engineer Blaine. He returned in a moment to say that the ship's engines were reversed and the propeller shafts revolving to the limit of the ship's power.

Nevertheless, it was only too evident that the Dewey was enmeshed in a treacherous shoal from which she was unable to extricate herself.

Officer Binns was ordered to throw off all possible ballast.

One by one the tanks were emptied. The air pumps were working valiantly but at each discharge of water ballast the officers of the stranded vessel waited in vain for the welcome "lift" that would tell them the ship was floating free again. The last ballast tank had now been emptied and the depth dial still showed eighty-four feet.

"Looks as though we were stuck, all right," was McClure's solitary comment as he gazed again at the depth dial.

The engines now were shut down, the air pumps had ceased working.

There was not a sound throughout the submersible, except the low

drone of the electric fans that swept the air along the passageways.

Every man waited in stoical silence a further word from his chief.

"Jonah had nothing on us," cried Bill Witt grinning, as the group of boys retreated down the passageway leading forward from the conning tower into the main torpedo compartment. Lieutenant McClure and his officers were conferring together over the Dewey's dilemma.

"This ship is no fish," ventured Ted timidly, his mind engrossed in the new danger that threatened.

"Well, it's a whale of a submarine, isn't it?" continued Bill in a brave effort to be funny.

Ted agreed, but was in no humor for joking, and hurried amidships to join Jack, who had remained within call of his commander.

For some moments the boys discussed the predicament of the Dewey, the unfortunate circumstances that had led her aground, and the possibilities of being floated again. Jack confided to his chum the fact that he had overheard Lieutenant McClure say the Dewey probably had ventured too close in shore and had run afoul of a sand bar.

"What's the next move?" queried Ted.

"You've got me, chum; I don't know what they will try next," answered

Jack, feeling a bit glum despite his natural cheerfulness.

Lieutenant McClure and his officers—-Cleary, Binns, and Blaine—-were now making an inspection of the Dewey fore and aft. As they returned amidships the boys overheard snatches of the conversation.

"Propeller blades free, aren't they?" McClure was asking.

"Working free and easy or else the shafts wouldn't turn," Blaine was saying.

From what the boys could gather from the conversation it was the belief of the ship's officers that the Dewey was grounded on a heavy sand bar. She had sloughed down deep in the miry sea bottom with her keel amidships firmly imbedded and her bow and stern floating free. The suction of the mud prevented her from rising.

In the wireless room Jack, Ted, Sammy Smith and Bill Witt finally came together and began speculating on the critical predicament of their ship. Cooped up in their cage of steel, shut off from the outside world of fresh air and sunshine, the crew of the Dewey were held prisoners like rats in a trap, dependent for life upon the air they were breathing and the precious stores of oxygen in the emergency tanks!

The next few hours were full of anxiety for the officers and crew of the stranded Dewey. Several times during the morning the ship's engines were set in motion and valiant efforts made to drag the ship off the shoal. But each succeeding effort availed nothing, except to eat up the precious electrical energy in the storage batteries.

In the petrol tanks was plenty of fuel for the engines, but it was useless here on the bottom of the sea where only the electric motors could be used in submerged locomotion.

Realizing the futility of these sporadic efforts at escape, Lieutenant McClure decided to wait until one o'clock for another supreme effort. It would be high tide at noon and he decided to make the great effort shortly thereafter on the thin hope that he might get away with the tide running out to sea.

The time passed drearily. Jack and Ted tried to get interested in a game of chess, but with little success. Bill Witt sought with mouth organ and banjo to buoy up the spirits of his downcast mates and succeeded poorly. Noon mess was served at eleven forty-five and even Jean Cartier, as he dispensed canned beans, brown bread, stewed fruit and tea, forgot to smile as usual at his culinary tasks.

"We ought to get away now if we are to get off at all," Jack overheard Lieutenant McClure say to Cleary after mess kits had been stowed and preparations were under way for the "big drive."

In a few minutes more the Dewey was primed for the test. Soon the clatter of machinery aft indicated that the engines were in motion.

"Back away!" was the signal flashed to the engine room. Instantly the full power of the motors was turned into the giant shafts and the propellors threshed the ocean with the fury of a wounded whale. With all the might she possessed the submarine strove to free herself and float away to freedom.

Thrice were the engines stopped and started again. But every time the quivering submarine failed to move an inch!

CHAPTER XV

THE HUMAN TORPEDO

"Looks as though we were up against it," remarked Executive Officer

Cleary to his chief as the Dewey's engines died down into silence.

Lieutenant McClure, his youthful face wrinkled in deep thought, looked up apprehensively.

"A very serious situation," he mumbled.

He spoke with marked gravity now, and there was no response from the executive officer, nor from Navigating Officer Binns, as they stood quietly and rigidly at attention, awaiting orders.

Inquiry in the engine room brought the information that the batteries had been greatly depleted by the tremendous exertions of the Dewey. The supply of "juice" certainly could not last much longer.

What next? Instinctively every man aboard the doomed ship was asking himself the question. It was only too manifest that the Dewey had run hard aground. The best that could be hoped for now was that the shifting currents of the sea might wash the submarine free before death overwhelmed her imprisoned crew.

"Make yourselves as comfortable as possible; we are not done for yet—-not by a jugful," essayed McClure bravely as he sauntered into the torpedo room where Chief Gunner Mowrey and his men were assembled in hushed discussion of the Dewey's plight.

Immediately "Little Mack" was surrounded by his men. They asked him all manner of questions.

"Remember first, last, and always that you are Americans and members of the United States Navy," continued their commanding officer. "We have air supply in the reserve tanks sufficient to stay here for many hours yet without danger of suffocation; and in the meantime quite a number of things can happen."

Despite their commander's cheery remarks there was little comfort in his words. Trusting implicitly their gallant chief, every man aboard the stranded submarine was keenly alive to the seriousness of the situation and mentally figuring on the possibilities of escape from the prison ship in case it was found at last impossible to float the vessel. The boys knew their dauntless commander, in a final extremity, would resort to heroic measures of escape rather than allow his men to be suffocated and overwhelmed by a slow death in their trap of steel.

It was now more than twelve hours since the Dewey had submerged after the exciting events of the preceding night and the air supply was still sufficiently impregnated with oxygen to enable the imprisoned crew to breathe free and normally. The boys knew that the Dewey could continue thus for at least thirty-six hours before her officers would commence drawing on the reserve oxygen tanks.

In an atmosphere of suspense the long afternoon dragged into evening. Every effort to free the vessel had been tried, but to no avail. Evening mess was served amid an oppressive silence varied only by the valiant efforts of bluff Bill Witt to stir a bit of confidence in his mates. Another and final effort to get away was to be tried at midnight with high tide. And then—-if nothing availed—-the boys knew full well that with the morning Lieutenant McClure would resort to some drastic measures.

Efforts at sleep were futile for the most part, although dauntless spirits like Bill Witt and Mike Mowrey turned in as usual and dozed away as peacefully as though no danger existed. Midnight and high tide kindled fresh hopes as "Little Mack" steeled himself for a last try with the Dewey's hardworked engines. Jack and Ted had spent the long evening in the wireless room with Sammy Smith, hearing not so much as a trace of a passing vessel. Eagerly they awaited the last herculean effort for freedom. At ten minutes to one the engines were set in motion again and the signal given to back away as before. Lieutenant McClure had resorted to the expedient of shifting everything movable within the Dewey to the bow bulkhead in the hope that the submarine might be tilted forward at the supreme moment. Now he ordered every man aboard ship, except the engineering force necessary to operate the engines, into the torpedo chamber forward.

"Whirr-r-r!" the roar of machinery reverberated throughout the hold.

The Dewey struggled again in mad convulsion—-but all to no avail.

The shifted cargo of humans and equipment made no difference; the

submersible remained fast.

There now was no doubt of the Dewey's serious dilemma. No spoken word was necessary to impress upon the men the critical situation. Sleep was out of the question. Jack rambled into the wireless room, where he tried to calm his restless spirits by rattling away on the key at the code alphabet. Lately he had been giving much attention to mastering the operation of the wireless apparatus and under the direction of Sammy Smith had been making excellent progress.

He nervously fitted the microphone receivers to his ears—-and the next moment sat bolt upright. He was startled to hear the clicking sound in the listeners that indicated the proximity of a moving vessel.

"Quick! Listen here!" he called out to Sammy Smith. The wireless chief dashed down the receivers and hurried to find Lieutenant Mcclure.

"Ship approaching from the southwest," said Smith hurriedly. "Coming up the coast and apparently about two miles away."

"Little Mack" adjusted the receivers and stood listening to the revolving propellers of the craft that approached and passed overhead. For a moment he debated the idea of releasing a torpedo that might be noticed by the crew of the unknown vessel. But such a plan was not feasible, for the ship would think only of being attacked and would stand ready to repel an enemy rather than look for a submarine in distress. Furthermore, such an expedient was out of the question; for, gazing at his watch, he found that it was only four o'clock and hardly light enough for a torpedo to be seen unless it passed very close to the oncoming ship.

"There is one thing we might do," spoke up Jack Hammond. "Lieutenant, I have a plan to suggest. We seem to be in a desperate situation that demands some prompt action. That vessel up there may be an American or British destroyer. It is up to us to find out while there is yet a chance for our lives. Shoot me out the torpedo tube, sir. I'm a good strong swimmer and I may be able to attract their attention. The thing has been done before and I'm perfectly willing to take a chance."

"Your proposal is in good faith, boy," interrupted his commander, "but it strikes me as a foolhardy proposition. We are down here more than eighty feet and, even though you got up to the surface, the chances of your gaining the attention of that vessel are mighty slim."

Jack stepped forward eagerly. "It has been done before and I'm willing to take that chance," he urged. "If we stay here we are done for. Unless we find some way of floating the Dewey within the next twenty-four hours we've all got to take our chances on getting out of here. Let me go now. It might as well be now as later on. We've got to act quickly."

For a moment Mcclure stood motionless surveying the intrepid youngster. It seemed such a desperate chance, and yet, under the circumstances, something had to be done.

"You are a brave boy, Jack," said Mcclure finally, springing forward and grasping the hand of his aide. "If you are willing I'll let you do it, for, under the circumstances, we are forced to resort to some heroic measures. God bless you, lad! And now let react quickly."

In short order the entire party repaired to the torpedo room forward where Jack was to attempt his hazardous experiment. Taking off his coat and shoes, which he fastened around his neck, Jack stood ready for the ordeal. Mike Mowrey had opened the upper port chamber and with the aid of his crew run out the torpedo that had been placed therein ready for firing. All was in readiness for the youth to crawl through the breech cap and stretch himself out like a human torpedo.

Lieutenant Mcclure was sure that the prow of the Dewey lay free of the sand bar on which the vessel was poised, and that there was no obstruction in front of the bowcap. But to make doubly sure he ordered the discharge of a torpedo from the lower starboard chamber. It left the bowcap free and with full power, giving assurance that no obstacle intervened beyond the mouth of the torpedo tubes.

Jack saluted his lieutenant, signifying his readiness to go.

"So longs Ted!" was his jaunty sally as he turned for an instant to his old Brighton chum. For a few seconds the two boys gazed full into each other's eyes, their hands clasped in a farewell.

"Good luck to you, old man!" said Ted, with a gulp in his throat.

"All ready now!" smiled Jack, as he turned first to his commander and then inserted his head in the mouth of the torpedo tube, motioning with his hands for his comrades to thrust him into the chamber.

CHAPTER XVI

IN THE WIRELESS STATION

In less time than it takes to tell, Jack was bundled into the long steel case, his arms stretched over his head well forward toward the bowcap. So tightly was he wedged in the aperture that his shoulders rubbed against both sides of the tube. Before climbing into the chamber he had hastily crammed a handful of waste inside his hat to act as a cushion for the water pressure against his skull that would be inevitable once his body was thrust out into the sea.

"Are you all ready, Mr. Hammond?" called his commander as he bent over the mouth of the breech cap and reached forward to give the boy a friendly tug at one foot.

"All ready, sir," answered Jack.

The breech cap was swung shut and Jack could hear the click of the mechanism as he was locked in by his comrades and they prepared to shoot their human torpedo out of the sunken submarine.

Now he was completely isolated in the dark, cold tube. The voices of his companions were not audible. It was a time to test the nerve of the most callous individual.

Whis-s-s-h! The compressed air came hurtling into the tube with a roar as of a mighty Niagara. It enveloped him and seemed pressing against his body like many tons of steel. Instinctively the lad inhaled deeply and gritted his teeth.

In another moment the bowcap was swung open and then came a rush of air that shot him forward at a dizzy velocity. As though driven by the force of a thousand tornadoes the boy felt himself, catapulted out of the tube and into the cold salt water that closed around him like a great wall.

His senses reeled and his brain was numbed by the terrible roaring that pounded in his ears. But he had the will to live and he began his fight.

He brought his legs into play and swam upward furiously. Would he ever get there? It seemed an eternity as he battled through the mass of the sea. His arms and legs were getting numb now; his lungs seemed torn to shreds and his head throbbed with intense pain.

And then, when he was almost lapsing into unconsciousness, his head shot up out of the waves, and the boy realized that he had reached the crest of the mountain of water!

For a moment Jack felt paralyzed in every muscle. Then, as he breathed again the cold pure air of the outside world, his senses came struggling back through the haze into which he had felt himself drifting and he was invigorated again. With a great effort the boy turned over on his back with his face to the sky and floated luxuriously, with arms and legs limp on the surface of the water.

Resting thus for a time, he turned finally and struck out with a bold stroke, determined at once to make note of his position. It all came back to him in a flash—-the unknown ship that Sammy Smith had heard working its way up along the coast.

Was it near? Was it friend or enemy? Would he be seen?

Jack lifted his head and scanned the horizon. It was early morning and dawn was breaking out of the sky. The first thing that attracted his attention was a heavy pall of smoke that hung over the water. The sea was rough.

Carried up on the crest of a wave he beheld the ship that the microphone had discovered for him in the wireless room. It was now a long way past the spot where the Dewey lay submerged and had passed northward, several hundred yards nearer the coast. Carried fifty or a hundred feet forward through the water by the force of the expulsion from the torpedo tube, the youth had emerged in the widened wake of the vessel. Apparently it was a German warship returning to its base in Wilhelmshaven after a night raid off Dunkirk or Ostend. It was hugging the coast fortifications now for protection.

Floating alone in the ocean, a mere speck in the water, Jack turned toward land. It was his only salvation now.

Tearing off his hat and with it the wet waste he had inserted as a cushion for his head, he struck out with long bold strokes. The fresh air and the salt water invigorated him wonderfully after the long confinement in the stifling atmosphere of the Dewey.

As he swam he thought of the boys back there in Uncle Sam's submersible and how they, too, would be negotiating this same swim very shortly—-provided they escaped as safely as he had.

Before his mind flashed also the picture of what might happen to him when at last his feet would strike bottom and he would make his way through the surf to shore. He knew full well that practically all of the Belgian seafront was held by the Germans. It was not likely he could go very far without encountering a Hun coast patrol. But he reserved to make the best of the situation and trust to luck.

After a hard swim he found himself in the surf and then his feet touched bottom and he made his way shoreward through the breakers. Fatigued by the trip, he threw himself down on the sand, puffing and blowing from the effects of his fight in the water.

As he rested, he heard the murmur of a skyplane's motors and turned to behold a giant Gotha machine heading up the coast. Stretching himself out quickly, as though to simulate the posture of a drowned man cast up by the waves, he lay wide-eyed watching the German birdman. Undoubtedly, it was one of the aerial coast patrol.

Five hundred feet above, it lazily floated along. It came closer and closer, finally flying almost directly overhead. With bated breath the boy on the sand waited for its passage and heaved a great sigh of relief as it purred onward in the direction of Blankenberghe without giving any indication as to whether its pilot had noted the body on the sand below.

Jack scrambled to his feet.

"Might as well find out what's doing here," he muttered to himself. He peeled off his wet clothes. One at a time he wrung out his garments and shook the water out of his long black hair. Then he turned for a glance around him. In front of him loomed the sand dunes, their weird shifting formations dotted here and there with scraggly underbrush. Down the coast the picture was the same.

Turning, the lad gazed northward in the general direction where he knew lay Holland and her neutral shores.

"That's where I go from here," he said cheerfully.

He had jogged along not more than a quarter of a mile when the coast line veered sharply to right, leaving only the expanse of ocean looming up beyond the stretch of sandy beach. Following along the curve in the coast line, Jack found himself presently on the shore of a small land-locked bay. The mouth of the inlet was barely wide enough to permit the passage of a good-sized vessel.

But neither ship nor human being was in sight.

"Might be one of the secret passageways used by the undersea boats," Jack mused as he followed the curving line of the bay away from the ocean.

Presently he came to an abrupt halt at a break in the beach where the rolling sand dunes fell sheer away to the mouth of another waterway—this time a small stream that wound its way inland through a tortuous channel. It was no more than two hundred feet across.

Jack realized this must be one of the canals with which the coast was known to be ribboned. For a moment he stood in contemplation of the sight. Now he was more than ever convinced that he had stumbled into a U-boat base. The love of adventure gripped him and he determined to press on.

For the next ten minutes he threaded his way along the canal bank. Suddenly, as he turned one of the snake-like twists in the course of the waterway, he found himself facing an old stone windmill that stood almost directly on the canal bank. It was only a stone's throw away.

Instinctively the boy threw himself upon the sandy loam. There was not a sign of life about the abandoned structure. In the peaceful days before the war it had, no doubt, been used by a Belgian farmer to water his fields.

But now Jack saw something that set his heart a-flutter. From the dome-like crest of the windmill stretched a number of wires tautly drawn and leading away to some point beyond his range of view. For a moment he contemplated the scene in silence with tingling nerves. Satisfied at last that his presence was not yet known—-if any human being was within the stone tower—-he struggled up to a kneeling position and looked beyond the windmill.

What he saw now was a ramshackle farmhouse apparently deserted. Up the side of the dilapidated building ran a great wide stone chimney that reared its head through the gabled roof like a leaning Tower of Pisa. To this chimney led the wires from the windmill.

"A secret wireless station!" exclaimed Jack to himself. "Undoubtedly in the hands of the Germans and being used by them in the direction of their U-boat fleets in the North Sea!" The boy's pulses quickened at the thought.

Like an Indian on the trail he wormed his way forward until he came at last within ten feet of the windmill. There was a window before him. Slowly and cautiously he drew himself up to one side of the casement and then peered in through the latticed shutter.

At a table, on which was spread out the wireless apparatus, was a uniformed figure. A helmet lay on the floor and the man's head was bowed in his arms. He was asleep. A lantern hung on the wall toward the canal side and cast a dim flicker over the cramped interior of the place. Stretching himself up on tiptoe, Jack surveyed the room, but noted not another person in sight.

Quick as a flash the lad withdrew from the window. His plan of action now was clear. He must get control of that wireless key and flash a message to the United States fleet in the North Sea!

Stealthily he began to circle the stone structure. Momentarily he expected to hear the challenge of a sentry; but he was not molested.

In a few moments his foot touched a large flat stone step before a half closed doorway through which the light of the lantern cast its flickering rays. Jack looked about him for a weapon of some kind and noted a long piece of two-by-four that apparently had been used to prop open the door of the wireless station. Stooping over he drew the club toward him and then turned to face the door and the danger that lay beyond it.

Fearlessly but with the lithe movement of the crafty panther Jack stepped across the threshold. As he did so the German wireless operator stirred in his sleep, lifted his head and gazed full upon the American youth. With a snarl of rage and a muttered curse the burly Teuton sprang to his feet and reached for a heavy revolver that lay on the table.

But Jack was too quick for him. With a long leap forward and a smashing blow he brought the heavy stick of wood down upon the head of the surprised operator. The German sank in his chair and slipped to the floor, the revolver rolling off the table with a loud clatter.

Pausing only long enough to note that his captive was completely knocked out by the blow, the Yankee lad sprang to the wireless and opened the key. Now he was grateful for the wireless instruction good old Sammy Smith had given him back there on the Dewey.

"Z-z-z-z-z-z!" the wires snapped with their message, as he flashed forth the code call of the United States fleet.

Would he be heard? Was there any vessel within range that would pick up his random call. For five minutes the boy rattled away and then closed the key to listen. What was his joy to get an almost immediate response. It was the U.S.S. Farragut, a destroyer, reporting her position and asking what was wanted.

In rapid-fire reply Jack related the sinking of the Dewey, gave her latitude and longitude, and urged immediate assistance.

"But where in the world are you sending your radio message from?" came the query out of the sky.

"In a German wireless station on the Belgian coast just about six miles south———-"

But the message was never finished, for at that moment Jack heard a slight movement behind him and turned to look into the revolver of a bulky German who, in broken English, commanded the American to surrender!

CHAPTER XVII

UP FROM THE DEPTHS

Back in the hold of the sunken submarine whence Jack Hammond had made his miraculous escape, stirring scenes were being enacted. Not a man in the crew but envied Jack in his daring attempt to get away; every man realized that soon it would be his turn. Either he must follow the example of the one who had gone or face the alternate of a slow and horrible death.

Ted Wainwright and Bill Witt were speculating on the fate of their chum.

"I hope he made it all right," sighed Ted after a long period of silence that had followed the discharge of the "human torpedo." Gloom pervaded the chamber of steel; every man was at the point of despair.

"He's a good swimmer; he proved that when he plucked 'Little Mack' out of the sea the day we ran afoul of that floating German mine," countered Bill. "If we are as near the land as Lieutenant Mcclure thinks we are, then Jack will make it sure as anything."

Chief interest centered in the wireless room where Sammy Smith was listening at the microphone. If, perchance, Jack had made the surface and succeeded in arresting the attention of the passing vessel, then the microphones would reveal the approach of the returning ship.

But, as Smith listened intently, the sound of the revolving propeller blades gradually diminished and the commander and crew of the Dewey knew only too well that either Jack had lost his life in the venture or had been unnoticed as he floated in the sea.

"There don't appear to be anything doing up above," ventured Mike

Mowrey as he glided up alongside the two boys.

"Guess not," faltered Ted. "We seem to be right up against it."

All hope of rescue was abandoned. For nearly thirty-six hours now the Dewey had remained under water. Her crew of men, breathing over and over again the same supply of air, were rapidly exhausting the life-sustaining reserves of oxygen. Little by little the precious stores had been liberated until now very little remained. Many of the men were coughing asthmatically; several were languishing in a dumb stupor from the fetid air.

Ted could not help turning his attention to the huge ventilator shaft that fed fresh air into the Dewey when she was cruising on the surface. He remembered well that first undersea dive back home in an American port when he and Jack had discussed the possibilities of ever being lost on the bottom of the sea with the ship's air supply cut off. Now he was face to face with that very situation. The thought chilled his blood and he found it very hard to be brave under the circumstances.

Jean Cartier, his face blanched and his hair ruffled, appeared in the torpedo compartment, the picture of dismay.

"It ees ze veery hard thing to breathe back there," he gasped, pointing over his shoulder toward the engine room aft.

Almost immediately the boys forward could hear Commander Mcclure giving orders to open the reserve oxygen tanks. Under the emergency measures adopted living conditions were for the time greatly relieved; but every man aboard knew this relief was but temporary and realized that in twenty-four hours more at the most the supply of oxygen would be entirely exhausted.

The morning wore on to noon and mess was served to a crew of men who cared little to eat. Grim disaster stared them in the face.

The meal over, Commander McClure called a council of his aides in the control chamber. It lasted ten minutes, at the end of which time "Little Mack" sent word to Chief Engineer Blaine to assemble all his men with the remainder of the crew in the torpedo compartment. One by one they came forward in response to the call until the entire crew was assembled. Then the submarine skipper stepped forward.

"Men of the Dewey," he began, in slow even tones, "I want first of all to thank every man here for the splendid work he has done since we left God's country. We have established a record that, whether we live or die, will become an essential part of the history of the United States. The crew that we started with is intact, save for one brave man—-Jack Hammond—-who, on his own petition, was the first to be shot out of our stranded submersible in hopes that he might bring us succor. What has happened to him it is impossible to say, but what he has done, you can do, and it is the only thing you can do." He spoke hopelessly. "I have tried every means I can think of to float the Dewey, and we have been unable to move so much as an inch. We are helpless—-foundered. We are breathing the last of our reserve stores of fresh air. By to-morrow morning they will probably be exhausted, and you know what that means."

He paused for a moment amid a death-like silence, and then continued:

"There is but one course open to us. We shall draw lots. Then, in turn, we shall attempt to make our escape while there is yet time. Each man may have his own preference; you may either go out through the torpedo tube as did Jack Hammond, or you may go through the conning tower. Each man will please write his name on a slip of paper and deposit it in this code book box. Officer Cleary will draw the names from the box and Officer Binns will read them."

Slips of paper were produced by the ship's executive officer and passed around the circle. Hardly a word was spoken during this procedure, the usual debonair Bill Witt slouching against the hull of the Dewey, a picture of abject despair. It took only a few minutes to prepare the slips and they were collected by Officer Cleary, who in turn deposited them in the code box. Captain McClure stirred them around for a moment and then directed Officer Cleary to begin drawing.

Every man in the group viewed the proceedings with a tense face. Not a word was spoken as the executive officer thrust his hand into the box and drew out the first slip and handed it to Officer Binns.

"Joe Sampson," read the navigating officer as he handed the slip to Commander McClure, who, with pencil and paper, was ready to write the names of his men as they were drawn. Joe was one of the electricians, a boy of nineteen from New York who had shipped on the Dewey with Jack and Ted.

The drawing continued until every name had been polled. Mike Mowrey was second on the list, Officer Binns third. Bill Witt was drawn as No. 7 and Ted as No. 16.

"But where is your name?" asked Executive Officer Cleary, turning to his chief.

"Little Mack" merely smiled and made no reply.

And then it dawned upon Ted, who suddenly realized that the name of his gallant chief had not been called in the lottery. "Little Mack" had purposely withheld his own name and meant to be the last man in the Dewey after every other man had gone!

There was a commotion in the excited group as various members of the crew sought to take exception to their captain's voluntary omission of his own name. But the young lieutenant held up his hand for silence.

"I am the captain of this ship and take orders, from no man," he announced bravely. "One man has to stay behind and I reserve that honor for myself."

He paused for an instant and then added:

"The first man will go out at three o'clock to-morrow morning. We shall have to get busy at that time before we have exhausted the compressed air that yet remains in our tanks. It will require considerable pound pressure for this job and we might as well be at it while there is yet time. As near as I can estimate we are not more than a mile off shore. Once afloat, I would advise each of you to swim for land and take your chances there. That's all."

And with a wave of his hand he dismissed his men.

The hours dragged on into the afternoon and evening. Some of the men crouched alone in their quarters, facing in solitude the impending ordeal; others conversed together in low tones debating how they would choose their method of escape. Bill Witt, true to his inherent optimism, toted out his old banjo.

"Old Black Joe," he sang, and all the old familiar home songs. And then, while some of the braver spirits were singing he swung into "The Star Spangled Banner."

Instantly every man was on his feet and standing at attention. Thus they stood until Bill picked his way through to "the home of the brave."

Yes, the "home of the brave!" Here were sons of Uncle Sam, wrecked on the bottom of the sea, exemplifying that bravery that has characterized the boys of our army and navy in every stage of our history. Not a man in the Dewey but was inspired by the grand old song and steeled to die bravely for Old Glory if necessary and uphold the fair traditions of the U.S. Navy.

From that moment the mental atmosphere within the Dewey was cleared. Inspired by the national anthem, every man resolved that now, do or die, he would perform his part bravely.

"Where do we go from here, boys?" Bill started to play, and immediately a dozen lusty voices joined in the rag-time refrain.

So the merriment continued over evening mess and into the evening. Ted had strolled into the torpedo room absent-mindedly and was leaning with one arm over one of the torpedoes in the starboard rack when suddenly there flashed through his mind a wild inspiration. Instantly he straightened and gazed about him. One at a time he counted the torpedoes in the hold of the Dewey. There were three loaded in the tubes and two more in the port and starboard racks.

"I'll do it, I'll do it," he shouted aloud and raced aft immediately to the control chamber where his commander sat writing at an improvised table.

Lieutenant McClure turned as Ted stopped and came to a salute.

"If you please, sir," Ted began, "I've been hatching a crazy kind of a notion in my mind. I'd like to offer it in the way of a suggestion, if you don't mind, sir."

"Go ahead, lad," said "Little Mack" with a show of interest.

"All right, sir," replied Ted. "There are five torpedoes aboard the Dewey. It occurred to me that you might load all four tubes. Start the engines and reverse them and then when we are tugging with all our might shoot out the four torpedoes one after the other in rapid succession. We'll lighten our load a lot and the kick of the firing may drag us off. That's all, sir, but it was just an idea and I couldn't help telling you, sir."

The captain of the Dewey sat bold upright in his chair.

"I never thought of trying such a plan. I'll try it—-I'll try it," he shouted.

"Little Mack" jumped to his feet and pressed the buzzer for his executive officer. In a moment Officer Cleary appeared and the plan was unfolded to him.

In quicker time than it takes to relate it, the Dewey's commander had sent orders forward for Mike Mowrey to load the torpedo tubes and for Chief Engineer Blaine to get his engines in motion.

"What's up?" cried Bill Witt as Ted came bouncing into the torpedo room.

"Wait a moment and you'll see," replied Ted.

From the engine room aft came the purr of the motors as the last precious stores of "juice" were turned into the engines and the propellor shafts began to revolve amid the hum of machinery.

"Reverse and back away at full speed," was the next order flashed to the engine room.

And then, while the Dewey was straining in every steel sinew, her commander reached forward and touched off the four torpedoes in rapid succession.

The little submersible seemed torn by an internal explosion. As each torpedo shot out into the water the vessel shook under the force of the explosion, rocking to and fro under the concussion.

"We're off; we're off," shouted McClure as he bent over the depth dial. The hands of the indicator began to spin around and the Dewey, relieved of every pound of ballast, shot upward like a rocket.

"Hurrah, hurrah!" the cry reverberated through the ship.

In another two minutes the American submarine had gained the surface, her hatches were thrown open and the men swarmed out on deck—-to life and freedom!

CHAPTER XVIII

IN THE RAT'S NEST

Trapped in the German wireless station with a burly Prussian at the other end of the business-looking revolver, Jack Hammond was completely at the mercy of his captor. For a moment the American lad debated in his mind the advisability of knocking the weapon out of the hand of the German; but he noted the forefinger firmly pressed on the trigger and knew full well the least show of resistance would take him out of life altogether.

"Where come you from?" asked the German in his best and gruffest English.

Jack declined to answer, but instead sat staring insolently at the towering figure. His reply was a shrug of the shoulders.

From the wireless operator on the floor came a low moan as he slowly regained consciousness. The fellow had been merely stunned. Now he rolled over and struggled into a sitting posture.

The two Germans conversed together for a few minutes in their own language. Jack, who had studied German at Brighton before the war, was able to gather from their conversation that the wireless operator was telling his companion of the surprise attack. Soon the wireless man was able to get upon his feet and as he did so glowered at Jack as though he would like to leap upon him.

Again they tried to question him; but he refused to answer their questions. This only angered them the more. The wireless operator shuffled over to a closet in the corner and returned in a moment with a coil of rope which he handed to his superior, who was apparently the officer of the guard.

"Sit down in that chair," commanded the German officer.

At that he thrust a revolver under Jack's ear and motioned with his other arm for the American to wheel around facing the wireless with his back to the door. Securely they bound him to the chair. His arms and legs were pinioned so tightly that the rope cut into his flesh. One of them now withdrew from the room and the other remained on guard at the door. Every once in a while the German officer on guard walked over to Jack and glared at him with a fiendish sort of grin; kicking at the boy's bound legs and brandishing his revolver in a menacing fashion.

"B-z-z-z-z," the wireless began to talk. But not for long, for the German on guard, who apparently knew little about the operation of the wireless apparatus, scurried over to the table and, after fumbling about for a moment madly and in haste, succeeded eventually in shutting off the key and stopping the flow of words that had been filtering in over the wires. But not before Jack, alert to the message in code that he had heard, was able to translate in part. As near as Jack could make out it was the U.S. destroyer Farragut speaking a United States battleship in the North Sea at something like seventy-five miles away. But now the wireless was stopped and the lad sat helplessly in the power of the enemy.

After about twenty minutes' wait Jack heard the sound of approaching footsteps outside and the clink of accoutrements that denoted the approach of an armed body of some sort. The sentry at the door came to attention and saluted the leader of a file of some ten men who halted and set their guns down with a thud that Jack could plainly hear in the wireless station. There was a short exchange of words at the door and then the commander of the detail stalked over and took a look at the prisoner. Jack looked up to see before him a brawny German in the uniform of a lieutenant of the Imperial German Navy.

"Who are you?" the officer demanded.

Jack shook his head in reply.

"How did you get here?" came the command more sharply.

Still Jack kept silence.

"Search him!" ordered the officer, and after a search that revealed nothing, he added in German:

"Take him away—-we'll go into his record later. He's only a boy anyhow, and boy spies are not worth bothering about in this man's war."

Jack was marched off to the canal bank and, following the towpath for a time, the party reached a small fishing village of not more than thirty or forty huts built upon the banks of a stream that Jack realized immediately was the same waterway up which he had made his way to the wireless station. Now he was a mile or more inland from the lagoon and the seacoast.

In the water, moored alongside a wharf, was a huge submarine—-one of the latest type of U-boat. This, no doubt, was its hiding place and the rendezvous of other U-boats. Like a flash it occurred to the American boy that he had penetrated, or rather had been escorted, into the heart of one of the submarine bases.

"If I ever get out of this mess," he resolved to himself, "I'll put

Uncle Sam wise to this rat hole."

Down into the village he was led and directly to the headquarters of the base officer. The party paused before a cottage that once had been the happy home of a Belgian fisherman. The German lieutenant tapped him on the shoulder and motioned for him to follow. In a moment Jack was ushered into the presence of a corpulent German naval captain with sleepy eyes, who looked without interest at the youthful prisoner and yawned as he heard the story of the capture.

"Shoot the wireless man who fell asleep," he drawled. "Lock up the boy for the present. I'm not in the mood to cross examine a young spy." And yawning again he waved dismissal.

Jack was conducted to an old boat house that in the days before the war had been used by the Belgian fishermen as a repair shop for their fishing craft. He was glad of a chance to rest. The ropes had bound his legs and arms painfully, and his muscles ached from the battering he had received in the sea while making his escape from the Dewey. The Dewey! Jack thought now of his good old ship and wondered what "Little Mack" and the rest of the boys were doing.

Completely tired out, he climbed into a dilapidated old fishing dory and stretched himself out in the bottom of the boat. Using a tarpaulin for a cover, he made himself as comfortable as possible and dozed off.

So fatigued was he that he slept soundly, unconscious of the activity without, where the moored U-boat was being fitted for another voyage into the North Sea.

It was several hours past noon when he was awakened by the roar of guns, hoarse cries of men, and the stamp of feet outside his prison. As he jumped to his feet and clambered out of the boat a shell burst just over the fish-house, scattering a hail of metal over the flimsy roof and tearing a jagged hole in the wall above the doorway. Running to a window that looked out over the canal wharf, Jack saw Germans scrambling up out of the hold of the U-boat, some of them carrying rifles, others lugging a machine gun. The village was in wild confusion.

"Am I dreaming?" Jack asked himself incredulously, "or is the village being attacked?"

For answer came another shell that ripped its way clean through the frame building in which he was housed, bursting with a roar that brought the flimsy structure crashing down upon the head of the imprisoned boy. Blinded by the dust and splinters, he fought his way madly through the mass of debris until he emerged clear of the wreck. The first thing he stumbled upon was the body of the German sentry who had been posted outside the guardhouse. He had been struck down by a fragment of the shell and blood flowed from an ugly wound in the head.

Jack paused only long enough to rip off the sidearms and ammunition belt of the stricken German and then ran pell-mell across the open space that fronted the old guardhouse to one of the village streets up which the stream of German sailors had vanished. As he got an unbroken view up the street and on to the higher ground that stretched away from the village, Jack beheld a pitched battle in progress with a skirmish line stretched out as far as the eye could carry. The Germans had raffled to the defense of their hiding place and had hurriedly thrown up an emplacement for their machine guns. "Crack—-crack——crack!" came the spitting of the rifles, interspersed now and then with the louder detonation of light artillery.

Whoever they were, whether English, French, or American, Jack saw at a glance that the village had been attacked. He thought of the U-boat at the wharf and forthwith decided that his bit in the spectacular drama now being staged was to prevent the escape of the craft. Hurriedly retracing his steps, he made for the wharf, running at top speed and drawing the revolver he had appropriated from the wounded sentry. As he came dashing down to the wharf he discerned a German at the quay-post endeavoring to cast off the towline.

"Drop that rope!" he commanded. The German turned, saw the approaching boy and the menacing pistol. He threw up his hands instantly.

"Now get aboard as fast as you can," commanded Jack, pointing the way over the gangplank, after he had relieved his captive of a brace of revolvers. Jack followed hard on the steps of the German and once on the deck of the U-boat, ordered the fellow below.

"Close that hatch as you go down and keep it closed," ordered Jack. "And if there are any more below deck tell them to stay right where they are. If anybody shows head above deck I'll blow out his brains."

Soon Jack was in command of the situation. Making sure that the submarine was securely moored ashore, he retreated again to the deck of the U-boat, drawing after him the heavy plank that had been laid down as a gangplank. The battle on the outskirts of the village was still raging with fury. Shells were bursting all around the submarine. Running to starboard, Jack took up his position directly behind the conning tower with the steel turret between him and the village. Crouching with a revolver in either hand, he kept sharp watch at the closed hatches for any attempted outbreak from within.

Soon they came, pouring in wild retreat down the village street toward the wharf, running pell-mell for the U-boat. At a glance Jack could see the tide of battle had turned against the Germans and they were being worsted. He resolved to stand his ground and prevent the escape of the enemy by way of the submarine.

On they came, a dozen or more of them, heading directly for the U-boat. The leader of the column, looking in vain for the gangplank, called to a companion and together they attempted to swing another timber into position. Leaning around the turret Jack took careful aim and fired. The foremost of the pair threw up his hands and dropped. Maddened at this unexpected turn of affairs, the infuriated Germans began raining a hail of fire at the turret of the U-boat. Shielding himself as best he could, Jack returned the fire, making a special effort to keep the Germans away from the towline ashore.

As he fired again at a skulking figure, Jack felt a sting in his right arm and at the same moment his revolver fell from his fingers and splashed into the canal. He almost despaired of holding out longer when with a great cheer the attacking party burst through the village and hurled themselves upon the remnants of the Germans making their last stand at the wharf.

Risking a glance over the top of the turret between the bases of the periscope poles, Jack was stunned with joy to see the familiar uniforms of the bluejackets and marines of the United States Navy!

CHAPTER XIX

CAPTURING A U-BOAT

The battle at the wharf was of short duration. Completely surrounded and outnumbered ten to one, the party of isolated Germans threw down their arms and surrendered. From his vantage point behind the conning tower of the captured U-boat Jack kept tabs on the struggle until all firing had ceased and he was sure the Germans had been completely subjugated. The cheering of his rescuers apprised him of the defeat of the enemy. Walking out on the deck of the U-boat, he pulled off his hat and welcomed his deliverers with a lusty yell.

His sudden appearance from behind the conning tower of the U-boat completely nonplussed his friends for a moment. The bluejackets wheeled at the sound of his voice and a dozen rifles were trained on him in an instant.

"Don't fire!" yelled Jack. "I'm Jack Hammond of the U.S.S. Dewey."

For a moment the blue jackets paused—-and then pandemonium broke loose.

"Hurrah, hurrah for Jack Hammond!" they shouted. Hastily a gangplank was thrown out to the captive U-boat and Jack ran ashore only to be surrounded by his fellow-countrymen and fairly lifted off his feet.

"We've heard all about you—-how you escaped from the U-boat and called for help from the German wireless station. Bully for you, Jack Hammond; Uncle Sam can be proud of you," cried a sergeant of marines, who was gripping his hand with a clasp of steel.

Through the crowd of sailors and marines at that moment came a slender lad who elbowed his way forward with the ruthless violence of a fullback determined upon a touchdown. Right and left he tossed the bluejackets until he had fought to the side of the rescued American in the center of the group.

"Jack!" he yelled in delight.

"Ted!" cried the other almost in unison.

Unabashed, the two old Brighton chums embraced each other like two school girls just back for the fall term after summer vacation.

"Gee, chum, I never expected to see you again!" exclaimed Ted as he released his companion from a regular bear hug.

"Nor I you, either," said Jack. "Tell me, what happened to the Dewey?

How did you get out? Where is McClure and all the rest of the crew?

How did you get here?"

Jack was so excited thinking of his old friends he forgot his own part in the stirring incidents of the last few hours, and his own injury, as he insisted on hearing the whole story from his old roommate. "I'll tell you pretty soon; everybody is safe and all O.K.," answered Ted. And then he beheld the blood dripping from Jack's wounded arm.

"Wait a moment; what's wrong here?" he exclaimed, lifting the arm tenderly and disclosing to the view of the excited group of Americans a wound just above the wrist.

"Oh, it's just a scratch on the arm; one of the Boches nipped me while I was out there on the U-boat deck waiting for you fellows to come down through the village," he replied lightly, trying to minimize his injury.

A first-aid kit was produced and the wound hurriedly dressed. It seemed to be but a slight flesh wound. In the midst of the dressing a great shrapnel shell burst just on the other side of the canal and threw some of its fragments into the water just beyond the U-boat. At the same moment was heard the whirr of an airplane motor overhead and very shortly a hand bomb crashed to earth not more than two hundred yards up the canal towpath, exploding with a terrible detonation and tearing up a fearful hole in the ground.

"The German guns are all in action now," said Ted as he watched the airplane circling above the U-boat base.

Jack was soon told of the situation. He had been rescued by a landing party from several warships of the U.S. fleet. Under the cover of their guns, trained upon the German fortifications at Blankenberghe, further up the coast, and another Hun fort further down the coast, the bluejackets and marines had come ashore.

Seaward could be heard the incessant pounding of the American guns, intermingled with the boom-boom of the German artillery in the coast defenses. The German air patrol had flashed warning of the approaching American fleet and given the range to their gunners.

As Ted finished dressing the flesh wound, Jack saw coming toward him a naval officer whose epaulets showed him to be a Lieutenant-Commander of the United States Navy. Jack saluted formally.

"Are you Mr. Jack Hammond of the U.S.S. Dewey?" the officer asked.

Jack replied in the affirmative.

"I am Lieutenant-commander Davis of the U.S.S. Tallahassee," replied the officer. "You are the man we came after, and now that we have found you we must get right out of here as quickly as possible. I should like, however, to congratulate you on your remarkable exploit in getting away from the submarine and signaling so fearlessly for aid. Furthermore, I congratulate you, too, on capturing this U-boat single-handed."

Jack blushed and endeavored to stammer his thanks.

Immediately the American landing party prepared to retire. Deprived of all arms, the German prisoners were turned loose and driven out of the village, with instructions to get away as quickly as possible. After communicating with the American fleet offshore, reporting the rescue of Hammond and receiving instructions to get aboard ship as quickly as possible, Lieutenant-Commander Davis ordered the destruction of the wireless station. Likewise the two huge oil tanks at the canal's edge in which the Germans had stored fuel for their U-boats were fired, along with supply stores and every other thing that might prove of value to the enemy.

Lieutenant-Commander Davis hurried up and asked Jack whether his injury was sufficiently serious to incapacitate him for active service. When Jack replied that he was capable of performing any desired service, the American officer said:

"We shall certainly try and take that U-boat along with us. I am going to detail twenty of my men to the U-boat under command of Lieutenant Bridwell I should like you and Mr. Wainwright to assist Lieutenant Bridwell in getting the U-boat out to sea. We shall retire overland to our boats on the coast and leave you men to bring out the submarine."

Forthwith a crew was made up for the U-boat out of the landing party. Three Germans who still remained cowering within the conning tower of the submarine submitted quietly to capture. Lieutenant Bridwell decided to make the Germans assist in getting the U-boat out to sea.

"Put one of our men over each of the chaps and tell them to shoot at the first sign of any funny business," was Bridwell's order to Jack. It was found that the U-boat's fuel tanks had been but recently replenished—-in fact, the submarine bad been fitted for another cruise and was all ready to put to sea.

Jack found himself acting as executive officer to Lieutenant Bridwell in the operation of the submersible. Her oil engines were easily set in motion and her steering apparatus; was not unlike that of the Dewey, so the task of navigating the captured prize out to sea seemed not a difficult one.

Lieutenant Bridwell summoned one of the German prisoners before him.

"You understand English?" he asked.

"Yes," answered the captive Teuton.

"Then listen to me," went on the American commander. "Either you assist us to get out to sea or forfeit your life. I don't mean by that that we will kill you. The channel out to sea is probably mined and netted. If we explode a mine or run into a net and get stranded you die with the rest of us. Which will it be?"

The German signified his willingness to assist. He knew the channel very well, he continued, and would do his part. And then the most surprising thing happened. Of his own free will the captive told how he and his two companions aboard the U-boat had been pressed into the submarine service against their will. They had not desired to embark with one of the undersea fleet, but had been compelled to enlist in the service.

Many of the Germans were in open revolt against U-boat service, said the Teuton, because of the great number of submersibles being sunk by the allied navies. Only the previous week a revolt had occurred in the fleet at Cuxhaven, an admiral and a naval commander had been thrown overboard and a number of U-boats were lying inactive at their bases because of the inability to ship crews.

When the American lad had driven them inside the U-boat at the approach of the victorious landing party, continued the loquacious prisoner, they had decided at first to cripple the U-boat. But after talking it over they had decided that it would be better to fall into the hands of the Americans than to lose their lives by sinking the U-boat.

And now they were willing to assist their captors in getting safely out to sea.

Lieutenant Bridwell smilingly accepted the offer, but with a knowing wink to Jack which meant that the latter was to keep close watch over the talkative and seemingly docile German.

Now the evacuation of the U-boat base was under way. Having razed the place completely, Lieutenant-commander Davis was directing the retreat of his men over the sand dunes to their waiting boats on the beach front a mile or so off. German airplanes were making valiant efforts to wipe out the American landing party, but were so hard pressed by the heavy fire from the American battleships at sea that their aim was inaccurate.

The U-boat got under way with Lieutenant Bridwell, Jack, and the German pilot in the conning tower. Ted was dividing his time between the engine room and the control chamber, where the other two Germans were stationed under strong guard.

Moving very slowly, the U-boat was headed down the canal and very soon emerged into the bay that Jack had found in his exploration of the coast. In full view now was the American fleet from which the landing party had been set ashore—-the battleship Tallahassee, the cruisers Detroit and Raleigh, the destroyer Farragut and the submarine Dewey. The Tallahassee was lying broadside of the coast with all her monster fourteen-inch guns ready for action.

Soon the U-boat had wormed its way safely out into the open sea and was skimming along under the heavy fire of the fleet that was being directed against the German coast fortifications. As the U-boat, with the Stars and Stripes flaunting astern, moved outward, the fleet got under way.

Notwithstanding the heavy German fire from the coast defenses the American ships got safely away virtually unscarred in the battle. Fifteen miles out at sea the captured German U-boat came up with the Dewey. Jack had a joyous reunion with "Little Mack," Cleary and Binns, Bill Witt, Mike Mowrey and all his other friends aboard the reclaimed American submarine. And then he heard the complete story of his rescue.

No sooner had the Dewey appeared upon the, surface, following the successful consummation of Ted Wainwright's plan, than she had sighted the destroyer Farragut. The latter had heard Jack's call for help from the German wireless station ashore and had come dashing to the rescue. At first the commander of the Farragut had considered the whole thing a ruse on the part of the Germans to lure an American ship to its doom within range of the powerful coast guns; but the continued silence of the wireless station after that first frantic call for help had convinced the destroyer's commander that the message was genuine.

Along the way, while still attempting to speak the wireless operator ashore, the Farragut had picked up the battleship Tallahassee and enlisted its aid. The latter had summoned the Detroit and the Raleigh. It was while the Farragut was searching for some trace of the sunken Dewey that the escaped submarine had suddenly shot to the surface within a half mile of the destroyer.

When the Tallahassee, the Detroit and the Raleigh had come up, there had been a conference and then the landing party had been resolved upon. Two hundred and fifty bluejackets and marines had successfully accomplished the landing and after a brief search had spotted the wireless station and the U-boat village. The German submarine base, it was noted, was located along the banks of a canal leading into the coast town of Blankenberghe—-a waterway the Germans: had opened up after their occupation of Belgium.

Jack Hammond got a rousing reception. The story of his escape from the Dewey and his bold adventure in the German wireless station had become known and he was roundly cheered. When it was seen that the Americans had brought back with them a huge German U-boat there was great jubilation.

The captain of the Tallahassee, who was the ranking officer of the assembled fleet, decided that the Farragut should tow the captured U-boat to the American naval base on the English coast, while the Dewey also was to return to the same port for thorough inspection and repairs. A number of her crew were in bad shape from the long confinement in the stranded sub.

"Your men need a bit of play after their hazardous experience," was the message flashed to the Dewey from the Tallahassee's commander as he bade "Little Mack" and his men Godspeed.

And so, after an uneventful run across the North Sea, the Dewey came back to England, bringing as her prize a monster U-boat of the latest design, complete in every detail and ready for service under the Stars and Stripes.

And with her came Jack Hammond—-a new American naval hero, whose deeds had fitted him for rank among the immortal list.

CHAPTER XX

THE MOTHER SHIP

News of the capture of the German U-boat had preceded the returning squadron and a great reception was accorded the American submarine and its gallant crew as it came to anchor again in the harbor at Chatham. Several American warships were at anchor with other units of the British and French fleets, and thousands of sailors lined the decks to cheer the plucky Dewey as it wended its way to its anchorage, accompanied by the destroyer Farragut, the latter towing the captive German submarine.

During the days that followed, Jack and Ted found themselves lionized wherever they went while on shore duty. News of the capture had spread throughout England and France, and the censors had permitted a generous account of the affair to be forwarded by cable to the United States.

Letters and messages reached the boys, but none that pleased them more, amid all the adulation heaped upon them, than a simple cablegram of a few words, forwarded from Brighton Academy that read: "Hearty congratulations. We knew you would make good, and we are proud of you." "The Brighton Boys."

Closer inspection of the captured U-boat by American and English naval officers proved it to be one of the very latest and improved types of German undersea craft. It was a vessel of a thousand tons displacement and more than three hundred feet long, capable of a surface speed of twenty knots an hour and propelled by twin engines of eight thousand horsepower. The hull was constructed of double steel—-virtually one hull within another—-and the space between hulls given over to the storage of fuel oil, thus increasing the cruising radius of the vessel by permitting the carrying of more fuel. The periscopes were of the telescopic variety that could be raised and lowered.

"What do you suppose they will do with our prize?" asked Jack one afternoon about a week after they had returned from their adventurous voyage. He was talking to "Little Mack," who was supervising some repairs to the Dewey.

The submarine commander's eyes twinkled. "I reckon they'll turn her right in against the Germans," was his reply.

"Do you suppose they will man her with a crew from the American fleet?" pursued Jack.

"Haven't the least doubt of it," answered his chief. "Some of my boys may be taken to fill up her crew and I wouldn't be a bit surprised if they light on you.

"But not with my permission," continued McClure after a pause.

Jack was pleased at the compliment and hastened to assure his commander that he hoped always to remain with him for the war. Jack's brave fight to save his captain from the sea in the encounter with the floating mine, together with the experiences they had shared the last two weeks, had endeared these two to each other, and while there was a difference of some ten years in their ages, they were close friends.

Commander McClure's surmises as to the disposition of the U-boat were correct, as subsequent events showed. Chief Engineer Blaine and his staff of the Dewey were assigned to the U-boat with orders to familiarize themselves with the operation of the vessel as quickly as possible. American deck guns were being substituted for the German guns and alterations being made in the torpedo tubes to accommodate made-in-america torpedoes.

Returning to the naval station one afternoon from shore-leave, Commander McClure drew Jack aside to announce briefly that he had just received orders transferring him from the Dewey to command of the U-boat. Executive Officer Cleary, with a portion of the Dewey's crew, had been detailed to remain in Chatham with the American submarine. It was to undergo extensive repairs after its perilous adventure on the bottom of the sea.

"And now I have a surprise for you," smiled "Little Mack," as he took from his inner pocket an official-looking envelope and handed it to Jack. The latter took the proffered envelope and tore it open. What he read therein was enough to make any ambitious young American submarine sailor open his eyes.

It was an official order announcing the appointment of Jack as an ensign with an assignment to the captured U-boat as executive officer under Lieutenant-commander McClure!

Jack could scarce believe what he read and was so dumbfounded he could not speak for some minutes.

"And our friend Wainwright is to be with us, too," continued McClure.

"You mean Ted Wainwright?" asked Jack.

"Yes, he will be my aide and relieve the wireless operator at times," explained "Little Mack." "As a matter of fact," he continued, "I will ship the most of my old crew on the U-boat. The Dewey will be out of service for some time and Cleary will probably take her out on her next voyage with a brand new crew."

Jack excused himself in a few minutes to hurry away and acquaint Ted with the news. He found his chum writing letters and broke the news to him. The two did a fine young hornpipe dance, so delighted were they over the fact that they had been assigned together to the same vessel again—-and to the famous U-boat.

The next ten days were taken up by the new officers of the U-boat in acquainting themselves thoroughly with the operation of the captured craft, and in preparations for the new trip to sea. Latest news from the front had shown the Allies closing in on the German naval bases along the North Sea front. The combined armies of the Americans, the French and the British under one commander had driven the Huns northward till Zeebrugge was in danger of being wrested from them. Consequently, the American lads were anxious to get into the fray with their powerful new vessel.

"What are they going to call our new Kaiser-buster?" asked Jack of his chief one morning while they were inspecting the ship's storage tanks.

"So far as the Germans are concerned she is still the U-91," said the little captain. "You notice that we haven't changed the outside dress of her a single bit. Unless I lose my guess we are going to get pretty close to the Boche with this old boat of theirs."

And then "Little Mack" confided to Jack that the German code book had been captured with the U-boat, and that, furthermore, the U-91 had shipped as her wireless chief a former secret-service chap, Hal Bonte, who had worked for a time in the offices of a German-American steamship line in New York and knew the German language "like a breeze."

"Of course the U-91 has been re-named," continued the captain. "She will be known hereafter in the navy department records as the Monitor. You remember what that other Monitor did."

And Jack, of course, recalled at once the famous battle in Hampton Roads during the Civil War when the little cheesebox of John Ericsson had whipped the much touted Merrimac after the Confederate terror had completely dominated the Federal fleet and for a time wrested the prestige of the sea from the Union.

"Pretty good record to live up to," commented Jack as he recalled the feats of the famous little Ironsides that had saved the day for the Union.

"And you bet we'll do it," retaliated his chief.

It was not long before the Monitor was ready to put to sea again. Thoroughly equipped, her captain and crew familiarized with the operation of their new craft after a number of trial trips in English waters, she awaited only the call of duty that would send her forth for daring exploits against the Hohenzollern navy—-a German submarine born of steel out of the great Krupp works and put together in the yards at Wilhelmshaven turned against her own sister ships under the direction of a doughty Yankee crew!

At last came the order to move, an order received with great acclaim down in the hold of the massive steel structure where her crew of forty-two men laid wagers on the number of ships they would sink, and up in the conning tower where her officers fretted to be loose again in the North Sea. The Monitor carried eight torpedoes and several tons of shells for her deck guns, while her fuel tanks had enough oil to keep her afloat for many days.

During the next few weeks the world was startled by the exploits of some daredevil sort of a submarine that seemed to have an uncanny habit of turning up right in the heart of German fleets. Units of the German navy were being sunk with ridiculous ease. U-boat bases were raided and upon one occasion the mystery submarine had worked its way into a German harbor and blown up a cruiser.

Late one afternoon, just before dusk, the Monitor fell in with a submarine of unusual length and depth, a monster vessel of the type of the famous Deutschland that had made the memorable transatlantic voyage earlier in the war, but of even greater displacement.

Running partly submerged the Monitor had sighted the big fellow several miles astern. Jack was in the conning tower at the wheel when he noticed the U-boat across the water.

"Looks like an undersea cargo boat," said Jack after he had reported to McClure, and the two stood gazing intently at it through the periscopes.

"The Germans aren't trading with cross-atlantic nations any more," said "Little Mack" with a grim smile. "Most likely she is a mother ship for submarines. She has her wireless antenna up and is talking to some one. Suppose we go above and get in communication with her."

Accordingly, the engines were slowed down and the Monitor ascended until she was awash. In that position her wireless aerials, telescopically arranged like her periscopes, were run out and the wires strung.

Almost immediately she "cut in" on the big submersible.

At that moment the latter vessel spoke the Monitor and wanted to know who she was.

"Tell him the U-108 out of Zeebrugge," the American skipper told his wireless chief.

The message, in German code, was clicked out by Hal Bonte.

For a few minutes the two ships flung their wave lengths at each other and then the Monitor's operator closed the key to say to his chief:

"That chap over there is the Bergerhof, mother ship of the German U-boat fleet with supplies of fuel and food for our enemy's submarines. She is keeping a tryst here with her children and expects them at this rendezvous within the next two hours. After which the well-filled children are to visit the English channel and attack a group of transports scheduled for convoy to France the following night. She signals us to heave to and wait the appointed time."

McClure chuckled at the announcement.

"Just as I thought. Give them an O.K. in your best German," was his rejoinder.

CHAPTER XXI

Gain the Monitor spoke the Bergerhof and received in turn a summons to come alongside and take on fresh stores of fuel.

"If we do we will disclose our identity and it will be all off," said

"Little Mack" in a quandary.

Then Jack had an inspiration.

"Tell them we are having some trouble with our diving rudders and will be along shortly," he offered.

"Little Mack" seized upon the suggestion and acted promptly. In code the mother submarine answered that she was coming to aid. "Let her come; we'll give her a hot reception," said McClure grimly.

As the Bergerhof neared them McClure submerged a little and jockeyed his vessel into position for a sure shot.

This aroused the suspicions of the German and she asked whether the steering apparatus of the U-los had again gone wrong.

"Here is our answer," exclaimed McClure, and catching the big submersible full on the sight of the periscope glass, he released a torpedo.

Their suspicions now fully confirmed the Germans sought vainly to get their vessel under way; but the movement came too late, as the torpedo from the Monitor cleft the waters like an arrow and buried its nose against the hull of the gigantic mother ship just abaft the conning tower. With a mighty roar and a flash that illumined the night the speeding projectile crashed through the hull of the Bergerhof and rent the vessel like so much paper.

"Seems like a pity to put them out of business, don't it?" said

McClure with a tone of wistful regret as he surveyed the picture.

Jack was viewing the whole spectacle through the periscope, his chief

at the observation port in the conning tower.

"We sure did get them," commented Jack. There wasn't the least possibility of the mother ship offering resistance, since it was now a matter of a few minutes at the longest until she would be taking her last dive. So the conning tower of the Monitor was opened and the officers climbed on deck to watch the death struggle of the Bergerhof. The Monitor's torpedo had done its work well, for it was quite evident, as the American craft drew near the scene of the explosion, that the German vessel had been blown out of the water.

"Probably a half dozen men were out on deck when we hit them," said McClure. "Suppose we get right up close and see whether we can fish a few of them out of the water."

He rang the Monitor ahead directly for the spot where the German ship had disappeared under the waves, and as it drew closer slowed down the engines.

"There's one poor chap directly off the port bow," observed Jack as he pointed to a bobbing figure in the water. The Monitor was stopped and in a few minutes the unlucky German was hauled on deck. He proved to be a petty officer, suffering several slight wounds, and he grasped eagerly the rope extended to him by several of the American sailors. In like fashion six other Teutons were hauled out of the water, among them the captain of the doomed ship.

"We thought you were friends and not enemies," said the German executive as he looked first from McClure to Jack and then ran his eye along the deck of the Monitor, with surprise written in every feature.

"Sorry, but we had to sink you," was Commander McClure's rejoinder.

The prisoners were hurried below deck and made comfortable. They were a sorry looking lot after their narrow escape from death. McClure debated with Jack for a time just what to do with the prisoners, but decided finally to keep them until he could deliver them to a larger unit of the U.S. fleet. In the meantime they were herded into the spacious men's quarters just forward of the control chamber and a strong guard posted over them in charge of Bill Witt.

"If they start any funny business in here, they'll find themselves worse off than if they had gone down with 'mother' to the bottom of the deep blue sea," volunteered Bill as he assumed charge of his wards.

Anxious now to inform the Allies' fleet of the intended U-boat raid planned for the following evening McClure decided upon a flying trip down the Belgian coast during the night and then a dash across the North Sea to intercept speedy American destroyers and convey to them the valuable information that it might be relayed to the flagship and the warning given in due time.

"We'll stick to the coast for the next six hours," said the Monitor's captain to his executive officer, "and may be able to lay out another U-boat hurrying to the tryst with Mother Bergerhof."

Cruising on the surface the Monitor settled down for the night's run with Jack in command while his superior officer went below for a few hours' rest. It was a calm moonlight night with a smooth running sea and a breeze out of the south. Jack threw open the conning tower and climbed into the deck steering station. From his vantage point he had a commanding view of the sea for many miles in every direction and the young ensign reveled in the glories of the night.

Suddenly, at a distance of not more than two miles off the starboard beam, Jack spied a vessel driving leisurely toward the east with a trail of smoke floating along in her train. Taking up his glasses he was able to make her out plainly in the moonlight—-a destroyer!

Without calling his captain Jack decided to follow her for a while and accordingly altered the course of the Monitor to east by southeast until she was cutting in at right angles toward the speedy warship. After a chase lasting the better part of half an hour Jack found that the Monitor was rapidly approaching the mainland off to port, with the destroyer running into what appeared to be a convenient harbor on the Belgian coast. He decided to report to McClure before proceeding further, and forthwith sent Ted to waken the ship's commander. In a few minutes McClure climbed into the conning tower.

"What's up now?" he asked as he swept the horizon.

"Destroyer right ahead, sir," reported Jack as he indicated the position of the vessel. McClure picked it up with his glasses, and by taking the Monitor's position was able very shortly to determine that the vessel was off the entrance to Ostend.

"We might as well run up a bit closer and take a shot at her anyway," he announced shortly.

Crowding on full speed, the American vessel edged in closer and was then partially submerged. The German vessel had not noticed the submarine as yet; at least, she gave no indication of being cognizant of the proximity of the American vessel. At a distance of three thousand yards McClure decided to loose a torpedo.

"We'll take one shot and then dive," he said. "The coast is studded with guns everywhere here and we are too close to them to loiter around long."

In another moment, after sighting carefully on the fleeing destroyer, McClure gave the signal to fire and Jack sent a torpedo whirling from the bow of the Monitor.

"And now down we go," said McClure as he signaled to take in ballast.

Not waiting to note the effect of their fire, the officers of the Monitor sent their ship careening into the depths and went down to a depth of fifty feet with a greatly decreased speed.

"Guess we had better turn now and make for the open sea," said McClure as he grasped the rudder key to swing the Monitor around.

But at that moment came a sharp rasping sound on the forward hull of the American vessel and then a mighty ripping sound aft followed by a grinding in the region of the propeller blades and an almost sudden stoppage of the Monitor. McClure and Jack looked at each other, dismay written in their faces.

"Trapped!" ejaculated the little captain. "We are caught in a submarine net!"

CHAPTER XXII

YANKEE INGENUITY

There was no denying the fact that the Monitor had become enmeshed in one of the German wire nets.

Unmistakably the scraping against the hull of the submarine was that of the cables and chains that composed the net. Furthermore, it was evident from the manner in which the propellers of the ship had ceased their revolutions that they had struck an impediment of some kind. McClure and Jack both realized they had, indeed, run into a snare of the enemy.

For the next half hour the Monitor was put through all manner of maneuvers as her captain sought to extricate his craft from the web of steel into which it had dived.

"Seem only to be getting in the tighter," said "Little Mack" as he stopped the engines and from his chief engineer received a report to the effect that the driving shafts could be turned only with the greatest difficulty.

That which vexed the Monitor's officers most, however, was the knowledge that their capture was almost certainly known by this time to the Germans ashore and that it would be a matter of minutes until a German patrol or some other vessel in close touch with the wireless ashore would be standing over the Monitor awaiting the time when the submerged vessel must ascend from the depths and surrender. For it was well known that the submarine traps were equipped with electrical lamps floating on the surface that were illuminated automatically the moment a submerged vessel came in contact with the charged cables underneath the water. Thus the light would engage the attention of either a patrol ship or the lookout on shore who would soon dispatch a destroyer to the scene.

Discussing this phase of the situation, Captain McClure had just decided to make a quick ascension to the surface and take his chances on freeing the Monitor of her entanglements before a German warship could come up; but at that moment Bonte reported from the wireless room the approach of a vessel to port, coming up at full speed.

"Looks as though we are always running into hard luck," said McClure disgustedly.

Jack tried hard to see the bright side of the situation, but had to confess to himself that things did look rather black for the Monitor and her men. Nevertheless the boy figured to himself that surely there was some way in which Yankee wit and ingenuity could baffle the craftiness of the Germans.

"What are we going to do?" asked Ted as Jack joined him in the torpedo chamber.

"Haven't quite figured out yet, chum," answered his old Brighton roommate. "I'll confess that things don't look very rosy for us, but I'm not going to give up, nor will 'Little Mack' give up, until we have thought this thing over for awhile."

They strolled from the torpedo chamber into the compartment fitted out as the men's quarters and there came upon the party of German prisoners lounging in their bunks, chatting in their own language. Jack could understand one of them as speculating on the next move of the Americans. In their midst sat their captain, Hans Schmidt, from Bremen, he had told them. Jack paused and looked them over for a moment ruefully.

"I suppose they are chuckling to themselves over our luck and thinking how nicely they will escape when we go up above and hand ourselves over as prisoners of war," suggested Ted.

"No doubt, chum, and they probably have the laugh on us right this time," answered Jack solemnly.

But as he surveyed the prisoners again there came to him a sudden inspiration born out of the needs of the moment, a brilliant idea that sent him running into the control chamber and up into the conning tower where his captain sat alone trying to solve his problem.

"I have it; I have it," he shouted as he grasped the hand of his chief.

And then for five minutes the boy unfolded his daring plan.

"Little Mack" was so thoroughly convinced of the practicability of

Jack's scheme that he set about immediately to put it into action.

"The sooner we try this the better chance we have of getting away," volunteered Jack.

"Bonte says there is only one ship above us and it will be better to try to get away from one than from many. And besides, by going up immediately we stand a better chance of getting away with our plan of palming ourselves off as a German crew in one of their own U-boats."

And now Jack's plan was set in motion.

"Mr. Wainwright, will you bring Captain Hans Schmidt into the control room," "Little Mack" directed.

In a few minutes Ted returned bringing with him the captive naval officer. Then the American captain addressed himself to the German leader.

"Captain Schmidt, you are probably aware of the fact that we have driven into one of your submarine nets and are firmly entangled," began McClure slowly. His prisoner nodded assent.

"We do not intend to surrender, although the odds are against us," continued the Yankee skipper jauntily. "If we decide to remain down here and take our medicine you and your men whom we rescued so kindly from the mother sub are going to get the same medicine that we do."

He paused for a moment to let the import of his words sink home.

"But, Herr Schmidt, we do not propose to stay down here and wait for death to claim us," he continued calmly. "Life is sweet to us just as it is sweet to you. We are all here together, prisoners and captors, and if we live you live; if we die you die.

"Now here is what I propose to do. This, as you see, is a former U-boat of your navy that fell into our hands. You are a brave German captain and I am sorry to have had to sink your ship. But there is a way that you can save yourself and the men who survived with you.

"We are going to ascend in a few minutes. You are to open this conning tower and call out to the commander of this destroyer overhead that your U-boat has accidentally stumbled into this net. I am going to stand right here beside you in the conning tower with this revolver pressed squarely between your shoulders. We understand your language and can hear every word you say. If you decline to obey orders or make one false move you die instantly. You are going to direct your men here in the hold to work themselves out on the deck of the Monitor fore and aft. Mr. Hammond will go with the party forward, Mr. Wainwright aft. They will be armed, with instructions to shoot the first man who seeks to give an alarm. Your men will cut the cables and release this vessel.

"And now, what do you say? Either comply with our plan or stay here and die with us."

Herr Schmidt blinked for a full minute at the electric bulb over the compass. Then he looked from McClure to Jack and then at Ted, the trio of American officers gazing intently at their prisoner, grim determination written on their faces. He must have read in their eyes their willingness to die rather than submit tamely to surrender, for he turned in a moment to McClure and said:

"I vill do as you command."

McClure at once directed Jack and Ted to get down into the hold and change into the uniform of petty German officers, several such costumes having been found in the Monitor at the time of her capture. At the same time McClure ordered the German prisoners brought into the control chamber where he had Bonte, the wireless man, explain the situation to them in detail. Jack and Ted returned shortly and all was in readiness for the daring ruse.

"Remember, now, the first man who betrays us dies instantly," said

McClure as he gave orders to throw out ballast.

As the water was expelled from the tanks the Monitor began slowly to float upward. Moving over to the periscope McClure watched intently for the moment when the sub would emerge from the sea and he clasped in each hand a heavy revolver. In another moment the periscope had thrust its eyes out of the water and McClure was able to make out the outlines of a German destroyer standing on guard not more than sixty yards away. Pointing to the conning tower hatch, the American commander turned to the German leader.

"Now, Herr Schmidt, get busy," he said, with a wave of one of the revolvers.

CHAPTER XXIII

OUT OF THE NET

In stolid silence the German "Herr Kommander" signaled for the conning tower hatch to be thrown open and turned to find that Commander McClure had taken a crouching position directly behind him in the conning tower, a huge automatic gripped in one hand. Bonte had been summoned from the wireless room to overhear and translate to the American commander every word spoken by Herr Schmidt. The latter grumbled a reply with a nod of his head.

"Remember now, if you betray us, you die instantly," cautioned McClure as the lid of the conning tower flew open at the touch of a button and the German thrust his head out into the early morning atmosphere. A thin silvery mist floated over the water, and McClure, from his position, could see the, stars twinkling above him. The German destroyer hovered right at hand and her captain on the forward deck was bellowing a challenge at the Monitor through a megaphone.

There was a tense silence in the conning tower of the submarine during the parley that followed.

"Don't attempt to move," said McClure to the German at his side.

In whispers, at intervals in the German dialogue, Bonte translated to McClure the conversation of Herr Schmidt. The Teuton was telling his fellow countrymen that it was all a mistake; that this was the U-108 and that she had stumbled into the net by accident, having been pulled off her course by a defect in the diving rudders.

McClure had given orders that at the first sign of betrayal the conning tower was to be closed and the Monitor submerged again as quickly as possible. Ted stood by ready to transmit the order to lower away. But what was the surprise of "Little Mack" to have Herr Schmidt turn and shout down the conning tower in German:

"Send men on deck through the fore and aft hatches equipped to cut away the cable nets!"

Cramming his revolver into his holster, Jack hurried forward while Ted made off aft to the engine room. In another moment the forward hatch was thrown open and three of the German seamen emerged on deck, followed by the Monitor's executive officer in German naval uniform. At the same time Ted climbed up from the engine room on the aft deck, followed by four of the German prisoners. In the dim light the crews moved about their work like phantoms.

As best they could the Germans lifted the steel wires and cables and carried them along the deck of the Monitor; one toward the bow, the other toward the stern. It was tedious work and hard work, too, for the cables were heavy and so interwoven that it was a difficult task to move them. Ted and his crew had the hardest work because of the fact that the netting had become entangled in the propeller blades.

Jack and his men finished first, having lifted the last steel mesh clear of the prow of the Monitor, the Germans under him standing about the deck at his command as though but taking a little air on the deck of their own vessel After what seemed an eternity to the submarine commander in the conning tower, Herr Schmidt announced that the vessel was clear of the entanglements.

"Fine!" exclaimed McClure. "Now we are going away from here."

So saying, he rang the engine room ahead and the Monitor began to move off at moderate speed. At the same time there was a great commotion on the German destroyer and a voice at the end of a megaphone demanded in stentorian tones where the U-boat was going.

"Tell them we are going into Ostend," said McClure, as the German officer relayed the message into the conning tower.

Now the American officers were intent upon a safe get-away. In order to make as small a target as possible of the Monitor the tail of the sub was turned to the destroyer and in that position she glided away into the depths. In two minutes she was submerged, only the tips of her periscopes showing.

"They have their aft guns trained on us and are firing away as fast as they can load and reload," said Jack as he gazed into the tube.

"Well, they'll never get us now," exclaimed McClure as the Monitor took in another three hundred pounds of water ballast and dived down out of sight of the German warship.

There was danger now of running into another net and the officers of the sub were fully cognizant of their peril. As a precaution McClure stopped the engines entirely and then gave orders to submerge to one hundred feet. Slowly but steadily the vessel dropped away into the fathoms and was soon beyond the range of guns, depth bombs or other menacing projectiles. When at last the depth dial showed the desired depth the Monitor was headed straight out to the open sea and started ahead at eight knots an hour.

Unmolested, but feeling her way cautiously along until well out of the danger zone of nets and mines, the Monitor moved out to sea and set her course for the Strait of Dover.

By noon she had made excellent progress.

Not a vessel had yet been sighted, and with the freedom of the open sea the sub was able to cruise on the surface at full speed. Several hours later the Monitor picked up H.M.S. Chesterton, turned over the German prisoners, and gave warning of the intended U-boat raid on the transports. "We sank the mother ship of the submarines," McClure told the Chesterton's commander, "but they'll probably get their supplies elsewhere and try to pull off the stunt."

The world was electrified next morning by the news of a great battle between the Allied High Seas Fleet and the German submarine flotilla, in which the Germans, outnumbered and outgeneraled, were beaten off with the loss of several giant U-boats. The Monitor played a very important part in the engagement and had the satisfaction of sinking one of the enemy ships by gunfire, coming up at close range right beside the U-boat and engaging her in an old-fashioned hand-to-hand conflict.

Several days later while cruising in the North Sea a call came to the Monitor—-a radiogram from the flagship of the American admiral, summoning the sub to a rendezvous with other allied submarines for important instructions.

CHAPTER XXIV

INTO ZEEBRUGGE

The appointed time the Monitor arrived with other units of the American submarine fleet at the designated point off the English coast, to which point the undersea flotilla had been ordered by wireless. There, awaiting them, was the Admiral's flagship, and all around her trim vessels flying the Stars and Stripes—-"sentinels of democracy."

In the fleet mobilized the Monitor spoke several vessels that had accompanied the Dewey across the Atlantic on her first voyage into the war zone; there, also, were many other submarines built in American shipyards and now in commission in the North Sea activities. It was a wonderful picture well calculated to stir the blood of indomitable spirits like Jack Hammond and Ted Wainwright.

In response to a call from the flagship the Monitor came alongside and Lieutenant McClure with his executive officer and his aide went aboard. From the Admiral himself they received warm commendation for the heroic exploits of the converted U-boat, with special reference to the individual deeds of Ensign Hammond and Ensign Wainwright.

"Permit me to present you two brave lads with these," said the American Admiral as he took from his aide two official envelopes and handed them to Jack and Ted. Saluting, the two boys took the communications and stepped back beside their commander. The Admiral and Lieutenant McClure withdrew and went below, leaving Jack and Ted on the forward deck under the giant fifteen-inch guns of the battleship Pennsylvania, flagship of the American North Sea fleet.

The Brighton boys proceeded to open the official documents and found commissions signed by the Secretary of the Navy delegating to them the rank of first lieutenant, U.S.N.

Needless to say both boys were quite elated over their rare good fortune. It was, indeed, a moment for elation, considering their short term of service in the navy. Each had won his spurs in the great arena of service through devotion to duty and the flag and by exercising that rare courage and initiative that has characterized the fighting men of the U.S. Navy.

"I'm glad for the sake of dear old Brighton that we have made good, aren't you, chum?" asked Jack.

"You've said it, old boy!" answered Ted.

And then the lads for a moment digressed from the great war to talk of dear old "room 63" back there on the third floor of the dormitories under the campus oaks, with the lights of the town gleaming at night from the windows. It was the first time they had approached anything like "homesickness" as each confessed he would like once more to stroll up the campus and "see the boys."

Pretty soon Captain McClure emerged from amidships with the Admiral and after a formal exchange of courtesies the officers of the Monitor went over the side of the Pennsylvania and back to the submarine. Captain McClure was engrossed in thought and as soon as he and his staff arrived on the Monitor he beckoned them to follow him below.

"Very important news, boys," he began.

"The department has ordered a concerted attack on Zeebrugge. The allied armies have been making a successful drive in Flanders designed at getting in behind the German U-boat bases. It seems to be the consensus of opinion among the naval strategists of our own country, as well as in England and France, that the only way to stop the German submarine is to cut off the Germans at their naval bases. That is the aim of the land drive, and now it is the navy's turn."

He paused for a moment, and then continued:

"But now, to be more explicit. Here are the orders that I have just received from the Admiral, in conference with other American and English naval commanders. A picked fleet from the allied navies has been selected for the attack on Zeebrugge. Our American submarines are to lead the way. We are expected to worm our way inside the enemy port and open the attack, Then the battleships will open fire on the coast fortifications.

"I'll give you a bit of information that you probably don't know. In the Monitor when she was captured in the U-boat base below Blankenberghe—-thanks to Mr. Hammond's courage and initiative—-was found a complete chart of the approach to Zeebrugge. Mines, nets, and other impediments all marked off."

"We think we have the key to the situation in that chart."

Captain McClure—-who had attained that rank at the time Jack and Ted were made lieutenants—-further explained that he had been designated in command of the ten American submarines that were to launch the spectacular attack. He said he would give his attention almost solely to fleet maneuvers and leave the handling of the Monitor to his lieutenants.

"We will do our best, sir," said Jack, as he squared his shoulders.

The attack was to be staged the following night. Now for the next twelve hours or so the crews of the selected warships were carefully to prepare for the fray and to rest themselves.

The Monitor was put in tiptop shape. Tenders came alongside and gave her stores of fuel and ammunition. The giant torpedo tubes were loaded and the ship's full quota of reserve torpedoes taken aboard. The night and following day were given over to leisure hours. Jack and Ted wrote letters home and to school telling of their promotions and some of their latest exploits.

At nine o'clock of the following evening the submarine fleet received the word to be off.

The attack was planned to be started at one o'clock in the morning under the cover of darkness. Keeping in close touch, the submarines spread out over the sea like a huge fan. Behind them at a distance of five miles moved the supporting column of dreadnoughts, battle cruisers, destroyers, scouts and mine sweepers—-units in the great fleet bent upon the task of smashing the German stronghold.

The Monitor led off in the battle array. Copies of the chart of Zeebrugge, the original that had been found on the converted U-boat at the time of her capture, had been given to every submarine skipper in the fleet. Each had his orders for this all-important night.

"Here we go!" murmured McClure to his aides as he signaled his fleet of submarines forward into the fray.

Picking his way according to the German chart, he set a zigzag course. At length the officers of the Monitor knew they were closing in, and so far successfully. The submarines were running submerged with only the tips of their periscopes showing.

All at once there appeared in the sky directly ahead of the Monitor a line of red lights. A German birdman, circling above on patrol duty, had observed the wake of the periscopes and had touched off a night flare.

Like a giant pyrotechnic display the red globules floated in the air.

No sooner had the light appeared than there came the boom of a big gun on shore and a huge shell screeched seaward over the Monitor. Instantly the coast defense guns of the Germans crashed into action. And now, from the rear of the Monitor and her consorts, came the answering crash of the great guns on the mighty ships of the Allies.

The furious battle was on!

German aviators, having sighted the American submarines, were bending all their energies on wiping out the "invisible mosquitoes." Guided only by the telltale wake of the periscopes, they were dropping huge depth bombs at random. One of them splashed into the sea directly astern of the Monitor.

"We will have to act quickly now," urged McClure as he rang for full speed.

So far, so good; not a mine had been encountered. The Monitor was worming her way unmolested into the heart of the enemy stronghold!

Convinced now that he had passed the guardian line of nets and mines, McClure decided to dive and run for the inner recesses of the enemy harbor. Now down, out of sight, out of hearing of the big guns, the Monitor relentlessly pursued her course, flouting the danger that lurked on every hand.

At last came the moment when the commander of the submarine flotilla decided to climb to the surface and make an observation.

With every man standing to his post of duty and every nerve strained for the next move, the signal to pump out ballast was given and the Monitor turned her diving rudders to ascend. Soon her periscopes thrust their eyes out of the depths.

"Look! there, off our port bow!" exclaimed Jack to his chief.

McClure saw it, too, at the same moment—-a giant German battle cruiser lying broadside to the harbor entrance and every gun belching forth fire at the allied fleet outside!

Responding to the control of her commander, the Monitor swung off sharply to port and drove straight for the cruiser.

McClure's right hand groped for the torpedo button as he sighted on the German battle cruiser. He released a torpedo!

CHAPTER XXV

CHLORINE GAS

Confident of security behind the mass of mines and submarine traps spread ingeniously across the harbor entrance, devoting their attention almost solely to the artillery duel with the dreadnoughts outside, the German cruiser knew naught of the stealthy torpedo from the daring Monitor until it shot suddenly forward below the surface of the water, revealed in the glare of her own searchlight. But it was too late then to avoid the deadly missile and it struck home abaft the engines and directly at the after magazine chambers. With a great roar and the upheaval of a mighty column of water the torpedo exploded against the side of the warship. One carefully aimed shot from the leading American submarine had laid low a ten-thousand-ton cruiser!

"Quick, down we go!" shouted McClure to his navigating officer. The Monitor shot down now out of sight, and the helm was thrown hard to starboard. That one shot was sufficient to apprise the Germans of the presence of submarines and McClure realized full well he would be a marked man next time he showed his periscopes above water.

It was in mid-channel that the Monitor ventured to the surface again. The periscopes showed another vessel, a second line battleship of the pre-dreadnought type, off the starboard beam. Undaunted by the hail of lead slugs that splashed the sea all around, the Monitor swerved and ran straight for the battleship's bows.

"This one ought to settle scores for that poor old mine sweeper!" yelled the Yankee skipper as he sighted through the periscope glass on the wide target in front of him not more than six hundred yards away.

"Give it to 'em, Mack! Give it to 'em!" cried Jack.

Again, a torpedo leaped from the bowcap of the Monitor and hurled its ton and a quarter of steel gray mass directly upon the port bow of the German craft.

As the Monitor dived away again her captain beheld the battleship listing badly, going down by the bow at a rapid rate.

"Two strikes!" he exclaimed enthusiastically.

"Some night!" gasped Ted as he clutched the foot rail that ran up the side of the conning tower.

"And some battle!" responded Jack at his side.

With engines slowed down the Monitor ran along a hundred and fifty yards and then turned her nose upward again for another stab at the German fleet. As her periscopes cleft the crest of the waves again and she emerged into the arena of activity McClure caught sight of a destroyer off the starboard bow not more than five hundred feet away. A searchlight on the forward deck of the German vessel swept the water in front of the Monitor with a long white finger of light that fell in a moment upon the eyes of the American submarine.

"A destroyer driving directly at us at full tilt with all her guns in action!" roared McClure.

At the same moment he touched off another torpedo; but, in his eagerness for another "bull's eye" the American commander had fired too soon, and the torpedo shot past the destroyer, missing the mark by ten yards.

In retaliation, the forward guns of the German craft belched forth a salvo of leaden hail that followed the path of the searchlight's rays directly upon the eyes of the Monitor. With unerring aim the German gunners had found their mark. A sharp crash; a roar as the water above the Monitor's conning tower was converted into a boiling maelstrom, and the impact of steel against steel betokened the fact that a shot had struck home in the superstructure of the attacking sub.

"Our periscope's cutoff clean as a whistle," exclaimed McClure as he backed away from the tube through which he had been observing the approach of the enemy craft.

"Quick, lower away!" he commanded.

Shipping ballast in all her tanks, the Monitor began dropping into the depths.

"Look, look!" yelled Jack as he pointed to the steel dome roof of the conning tower.

In consternation McClure and Ted followed the extended finger to a spot in the steel casement where a jagged hole had been torn by a fragment of the German shell fire and where now a thin stream of water was percolating through the crevice.

"We've got to submerge, boys; that destroyer is almost on top of us now!" cried McClure in frenzied tones. "Get down into the control chamber—hurry!" he commanded.

Ted dived down the hatch as fast as he could scramble, followed closely by Jack, who observed by now a steady stream of water pouring into the turret of the Monitor and splashing on clear through to the flooring of the chamber deep down into the hold.

As Jack lowered himself away into the inner chamber amidships the Monitor was clutched suddenly by a terrific explosion that rocked the already crippled submarine with the force of a hurricane and swamped it as though by a tidal wave. She quivered under the whip of the mighty lash of steel from above.

The German destroyer, driving full speed at the spot where they had sighted the periscopes of the American tormentor, had crossed directly over the Monitor and dropped a depth bomb that had exploded nearly upon the turret of the doughty fighter!

A great gap was torn in the turret through which the sea swept in a torrent. Fighting madly for the exit hatch into the chamber below, McClure was dashed off his feet by the lurch of the smitten submarine and sprawled against the steel side of the conning tower. With the spray dashing in his face Jack had a fleeting glimpse of his commander, and by a superhuman effort drew himself back into the turret against the mass of water. Hurling himself forward, he groped about for his captain and found him finally on the floor of the turret. Exerting all his strength, he succeeded in hurling "Little Mack" down into the control chamber.

Blinded by the swirling water, the youth dived headlong for the opening in a mad effort to escape the flood and get below that he might shut off the crushed turret from the rest of the submarine and hold the deluge in check.

"Close the steel partition!" he yelled to Ted as he leaped for the opening.

His chum, grasping the air lever, rolled shut the heavy curtain, but in such precipitate haste that it caught Jack just above the knees and pinned him fast. There he hung head down with the water pouring in all around his body.

"Pull me through, Ted! Hurry! Pull me through!" gasped the young executive officer, as he winced in pain from the smashing blow dealt his limbs by the steel partition.

Grasping his chum under the armpits, with the water splashing in his face, Ted braced himself against the side of the control chamber and pulled with all his might. Inch by inch Jack's body was dragged through the aperture, Navigating Officer Binns leaping to the assistance of Ted and hauling away until finally Jack's limbs cleared the opening and the steel partition closed entirely, shutting off the volume of water above.

"Are you hurt, chum?" asked Ted.

"Yes, but don't mind me," came the reply, as Jack sprawled out with both legs hanging limp and useless. Gritting his teeth to stifle a groan, Jack drew himself up into a sitting posture. By his side lay McClure unconscious. All around them flowed water, working its way fore and aft through the submarine.

"Go aft, Ted; find out how things are in the engine room," directed the injured executive officer. "And you, Binns, make an inspection forward."

The two officers hurried to make an investigation, returning soon to report that the boat had not suffered from the depth bomb so far as could be ascertained except for the damage to the conning tower. Jack directed that the Monitor be submerged until she rested on the bottom of the channel. The vessel dropped away until it came to rest shortly with the depth dial showing one hundred and forty-two feet.

McClure, stunned by a blow on the head, sustained when he was hurled against the side of the conning tower, was carried away still unconscious to his bunk. Jack, his limbs bruised, torn and partially paralyzed, insisted upon remaining at his post of duty and directed the dressing of his wounds.

"I'll be all right in a little bit," he murmured in response to inquiries.

Ten minutes passed, twenty and then a half hour, while the crippled submarine lay inactive with a foot of water in her hull and her commanding officers seriously injured. And then came an added horror when the electric lights throughout the vessel began slowly to fade away into darkness. Chief Engineer Blaine came hurrying into the control chamber:

"Batteries short circuited by the saltwater!" he exclaimed in a tone of dismay.

"And that means chlorine gas," added Jack.

"Yes, we notice it already aft," said Blaine all righted.

The pungent odor of the deadly fumes swept into the control chamber as he spoke!

CHAPTER XXVI

THE STARS AND STRIPES

The salt water worked its way into the batteries of the Monitor the deadly acid was generated and the gas permeated the air. Gasping for life, half the engine crew retreated forward, covering their eyes and noses to escape the asphyxiating vapor. With bloodshot eyes Chief Engineer Blaine stumbled into the control chamber.

"Impossible to stay back there longer!" he exclaimed brokenly, addressing himself to Hammond.

"Any chance of putting a bilge pump on the water?" asked Jack.

"Not a chance in the world; no man can work back there," replied the engineer.

By now the gas had increased in such volume that every man in the conning tower base was choking and coughing. The only thing to do in such an emergency was to roll shut the steel partition shutting off the engine room from the remainder of the vessel. To make matters worse the lights throughout the Monitor went out, leaving the vessel in utter darkness.

"Every man out of the engine room?" asked Jack.

"I'll find out," answered Blaine.

In the darkness the chief engineer called off the names of his men, getting a response, one by one, from the electricians, oilers and machinists who composed his crew. Not a man was missing, but many of them were suffering from the effects of near-strangulation. Jack ordered the opening of the reserve oxygen tanks, and this gave the sufferers temporary relief.

"Come here, Ted!" called Jack out of the darkness.

Groping his way to where his chum sat propped against the side of the conning tower, Ted bent over the prostrate form of the ship's executive officer.

"I'm growing weak, chum," said Jack feebly. "My limbs are numb and I feel so cold. In case I go under keep the Monitor down here about half an hour and then take your chances on going up. Better to be taken prisoners than die here like a lot of rats in a trap. Do you understand, Ted?"

His teeth chattering with mingled fear and cold—-fear for the life of his old Brighton roommate and cold because of the falling temperature due to the cutting off of all electrical energy—-Ted answered in the affirmative.

"I guess that's about all we can do, chum," he added.

Ted and Navigating Officer Binns conferred together in the control chamber.

"Better to go up and take our chances on the surface than to remain here under these conditions," counseled Binns.

"I agree with you, Mr. Binns," replied Ted.

And so, after another ten minutes' wait, the two decided to empty the ballast tanks.

In another moment the weight of water filling the ballast tanks was being thrown off under the force of the compressed air and the Monitor lifted off the bed of the harbor. Striking a match, Binns leaned over the depth dial, watching the fluctuating hand that marked foot by foot the progress of the Monitor upward. To lighten the load as much as possible and counterbalance the weight of water in the wrecked conning tower Ted released the torpedoes remaining in the tubes. In a few minutes the indicator hand pointed to zero and the Monitor's officers realized that now their craft was riding awash with her deck fully exposed.

Making his way forward through the gloom, Ted sprang to the hatch and raised the lid. As the morning light streamed in through the opening a muffled cheer resounded from the interior of the sub. Vaulting up the ladder, Ted leaped on deck and looked around him. There to starboard, not more than five hundred feet away, loomed a giant cruiser. From her stern tailrail trailed a familiar emblem.

"The Stars and Stripes!" exclaimed the youth as his comrades swarmed up about him from the hold of the prison ship.

A glorious victory had been won by the allied fleets. All about the Monitor were warships of the American, English, and French nations. Reducing the land fortifications after a terrific bombardment, the combined fleet had "rushed" the harbor in the wake of their mine-sweepers, engaged and overwhelmed the larger units of the German fleet there assembled, and driven some of the smaller craft into the Zeebrugge Canal. Thousands of marines and blue-jackets, formed into landing parties, had been set upon shore and were now taking formal possession of the German stronghold.

"Hurrah for the Monitor!" the cry reverberated over the waters as the plucky American submarine was made fast alongside the U.S.S. Chicago and the story of her night's exploits became heralded about. Willing hands assisted in reclaiming the wounded and gas victims from the hold of the ship. Jack and his captain, the latter still unconscious, suffering from a severe concussion of the brain, were lifted over the side and carried to the cruiser's sick bay for their wounds to be dressed. It was found upon examination that the ligaments and muscles in Jack's limbs had been severely torn and the flesh lacerated, but that his injuries, while painful, were not serious.

Great jubilation reigned on all the ships. A band on the forward deck of the Chicago was playing "Stars and Strips Forever," while from a nearby British battleship came the strains of "Rule Britannia." Their last rendezvous on the Flemish coast wrested from them, the backbone of the German U-boat campaign was broken by the concerted land and sea attack. Several of the allied warships had gone down in the spectacular engagement of the night, but a notable victory had been won, and the boys of the navy were in raptures over their successful engagement.

Later in the day Jack was transferred to a hospital ship. All the allied wounded from the sea battle off Zeebrugge were to be sent to England. Captain McClure was grievously wounded. Jack would not be able to resume active service for some time, so his surgeon said, and would probably be invalided home.

In due time Jack arrived in London, where for a time he was a patient in one of the American-endowed hospitals. Within a week he was joined by Ted. The latter had been granted a leave of absence. Together the two young lieutenants took passage on a steamship bound for New York, and, braving the perils of the submarine-infested sea, crossed to their own dear old U.S.A.—-"the home of the free and the land of the brave."

And now we shall leave them. Suffice to say that after a several months' sojourn at home they returned again to the field of activity to resume their places in the U.S. fleet and continue in service until the end of the war, reaping new honors for themselves, their alma mater and their country.

Of course, before they went back to rejoin "Little Mack," Bill Witt,

Mike Mowrey and all their old seafaring mates, they visited Brighton.

It was late afternoon of an October day when the young lieutenants, spic and span in their uniforms, walked briskly up old Pine Street to the campus of Brighton. Many of the students were loafing about the campus awaiting the ringing of the dinner gong when the boys arrived.

Hardly had they climbed the gray stone steps leading to the campus, however, before they were recognized.

"Hurrah for Jack Hammond and Ted Wainwright!" the cry resounded. Word of their arrival spread through the dormitories and soon a mob of chattering schoolboys surrounded the two young officers. As the dinner gong sounded, the heroes were hoisted to the shoulders of their old chums and carried into the dining room. There they met all the "profs" and were compelled to hold an impromptu reception while the dinner waited.

The study period that night at Brighton was set back an hour. Brighton had her heroes at home, and she was doing them full honor. Many of the boys had enlisted in the various branches of service and were now "over there." But those who remained held a joyous reception in honor of the two whose stirring deeds had brought such signal honor to the school that had sent them forth.

A few minutes after ten o'clock, when all the boys had been rung to their rooms and lights were out, two young naval lieutenants stood at the foot of the campus, gazing back at the facade of the familiar old dormitory, its windows framing the heads of many youths who were shouting a farewell to their old friends.

The boys stood in silence contemplating the picture—-listening to the chorus of good-bys.

Ted was first to speak.

"I guess it was worth while, chum—-our going away to serve our country and coming back to get a reception like this," he faltered.

"And then some!" came Jack's answer. "For Brighton and for Uncle Sam!

That's us!"

THE END

Milton Keynes UK
Ingram Content Group UK Ltd.
UKHW050207070724
445042UK00012B/546